ESCAPE FROM
CHERNOBYL

ESCAPE FROM CHERNOBYL

ANDY MARINO

Scholastic Inc.

Copyright © 2021 by Andy Marino

All rights reserved. Published by Scholastic Inc., *Publishers since 1920.* SCHOLASTIC and associated logos are trademarks and/or registered trademarks of Scholastic Inc.

The publisher does not have any control over and does not assume any responsibility for author or third-party websites or their content.

This book is a work of fiction. Names, characters, places, and incidents are either the product of the author's imagination or are used fictitiously, and any resemblance to actual persons, living or dead, business establishments, events, or locales is entirely coincidental.

Library of Congress Cataloging-in-Publication Data available

ISBN 978-1-338-71845-4

10 9 8 7 6 5 4 3 2   21 22 23 24 25

First edition, December 2021
Printed in the U.S.A.   40

Book design by Christopher Stengel

FOR MATT, ALLYSON,
AND CHARLEY

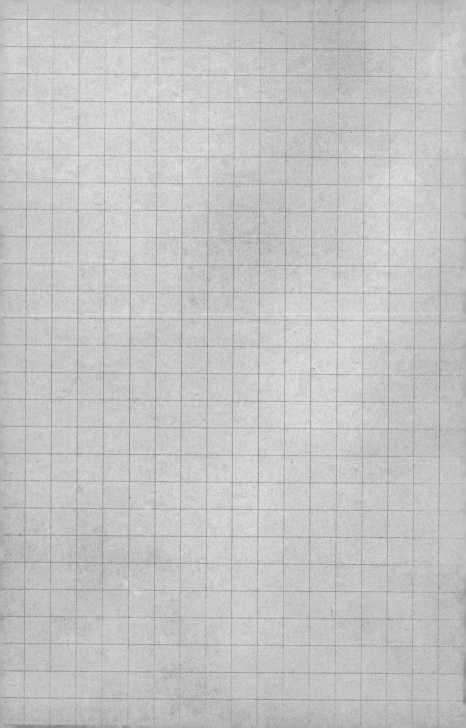

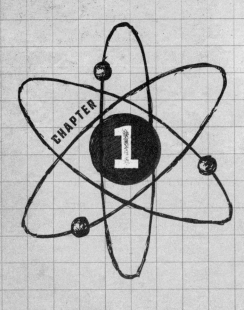

CHAPTER 1

Yuri Fomichev picks a wooden splinter from his palm. Months of mopping floors and wielding hammers have turned the sixteen-year-old's hands into the tough, calloused mitts of a Siberian oil worker. He flicks the shard away and grips the handle of his mop.

The only way to avoid splinters is to wear gloves.

Yuri refuses to wear gloves.

Better to toughen up. The people he respects most in the power plant—the *atomschiki*, the nuclear engineers who have risen to great heights, thanks to their brilliance and hard work—keep their bodies as fit as their minds. They box, run races, row up and down the river Pripyat, then grind out all-night shifts at the plant, taming the atom and bending it to the will of the Soviet State.

Yuri is the Moscow Engineering and Physics Institute's youngest scholarship winner. He swirls the mop's shaggy bristles through the puddle on the tiled floor with the same righteous fury and tightly coiled energy that drove him toward this goal.

Yuri had been seven years old when the Chernobyl Atomic Energy Station was officially connected to the Soviet power grid: 27 September 1977. Now, nine years later, alone in the endless corridor that connects the plant's turbine hall to its four massive reactors, Yuri can still hear the triumphant hymn sung by those first scientists, broadcast on State TV across the Soviet Union: *"For today, for today, current flows from the RBMK!"*

The RBMK.

Reaktor bolshoy moschnosti kanalnyy.

High-power channel-type reactor.

The national nuclear reactor of the USSR, twenty times the size of the American ones! That same TV show had taken viewers like Yuri, kneeling on the carpet in the living room of his family's Moscow apartment, on a quick tour of the glorious new power plant. The inner workings of the RBMK are a highly classified state secret, but the broadcast had been permitted to show fleeting glimpses of the polished marble stairs and stained-glass panels of Chernobyl's administration block; the sanitary locks where workers traded street clothes for white overalls, white caps, and white boots; the steel cavern of the turbine hall, all looming machinery and mysterious shadows; and, finally, the concrete vault that housed and shielded the reactor core, as big as Yuri's apartment building.

Seven-year-old Yuri had pressed his face nearly against the screen, convinced of several things at once:

His destiny had just been unlocked.

This five-minute TV special had opened up a wondrous new path that would take him far from Moscow.

The mysteries of the atom would rocket him into a glorious future, as if he'd been launched into the stratosphere like the man he's named after, famed cosmonaut Yuri Gagarin, the first human being in space and a Hero of the Soviet Union.

For today, for today—

For today I am mopping the floor, Yuri thinks. *Just like yesterday, and the day before, and the day before that.*

Yuri had floated through his first day at Chernobyl as if in a dream, moving through the very same sanitary lock he'd seen on TV as a little boy, donning the same white garments as his new colleagues and mentors, the technicians and atomschiki he'd spent his young life idolizing. Once he was dressed, it hadn't taken long for one of those atomschiki to puncture the dream by handing him a mop, leaving him stranded in a new reality.

Yuri caught on quickly to the rules of this reality.

At Chernobyl, *scholarship winner* means "intern." And *intern* means "errand boy, laborer, janitor."

Yuri oils squeaky machinery, prowling the catwalks of the turbine hall like a stowaway aboard some vast submarine, oilcan in hand. He patches up hairline cracks in the rats' nest of steel pipes that deliver cooling water to the reactor core. He delivers trays of potent coffee to the engineers in the control rooms monitoring the delicate machinery of the RBMK, catching a glimpse of the dashboards and panels, the dials and switches and gauges that stand between atoms controlled and atoms free to spark their deadly chaos.

But, mostly, Yuri mops.

Chernobyl is a leaky place. Yuri has come to think of it as a living creature with a beating reactor-core heart, and that creature—the monumental thing that looks so tough in its granite and steel—actually has a soft and easily wounded body. And from those wounds, many of them very well hidden, drip fluids of all kinds, from plain old water to oddly tinted oils to viscous, foul-smelling goo.

He lifts the mop from the puddle, sloshes it into his bucket, then presses the lever that lifts a plastic hatch to wring out the liquid. Such a simple and effective mechanism satisfies him. He splashes the mop back down into the spill, which is shaped like one of the lakes that claw Russia's vast interior. This spill falls into the "oddly tinted oils" category. Weird colors swirl and dissolve.

To occupy his mind, Yuri plays a game he invented called *where did this leak come from?* Where is this wound in the Chernobyl-creature? He also ponders a much more interesting question: Will this leak ever be fixed, or will he be dispatched to mop the same section of corridor, again and again, for no apparent reason?

Yet another mystery of Chernobyl.

He glances up at the ceiling and scans it for the leak's source. Nicknamed "the golden corridor," the 800-meter hallway is paneled in thin strips of blond wood polished to a high sheen. It's like staring down an impossibly long tube lined with rich gold plating, and the ceiling is no exception: more gold, interrupted by harsh overhead lights.

There, in a seam between the panels, is the sparkle of liquid catching the light. In his mind's eye, Yuri drifts up through the ceiling, to the pipes running just beneath the roof of the corridor, connecting the control rooms and reactors with the turbine hall.

Yuri studies Chernobyl's blueprints late into the night. He suspects that, if he were given the proper tools, equipment, and ten or so years, he could take the power plant apart and put it back together all by himself.

He notes the location of the leak. He will report it to a foreman, and the leak will either be patched or it won't, according to some political process that Yuri doesn't understand. The place where the splinter went in begins to itch and he rubs his palm against his white overalls. Whenever he thinks about the orders coming down from on high, which either get followed or don't, according to a *different* system of orders, Yuri's body tingles. The politics of grown adults are another kind of new reality, too shadowy for him to fully grasp—and in his heart, he doesn't much care to try. He feels a creeping sense of guilt, as if this silent thought is the same as actually *criticizing the Soviet State out loud*—

Which is what his uncle Pavlo does, every night, as he sips his after-dinner tea.

Yuri's knuckles turn white as he tightens his grip on the mop.

Uncle Pavlo is Yuri's father's brother, and he has been hosting Yuri since he's been in the city of Pripyat, interning at Chernobyl.

Yuri has never met anyone like Uncle Pavlo. He is a radio announcer, the voice of Pripyat's news station. All day he reads news reports celebrating Soviet progress—the launch of a new submarine class out of the shipyard in Leningrad, announcements from the Kremlin—plus news of American failures. Pavlo's voice is comforting and familiar to the citizens of Pripyat. Yuri has witnessed total strangers greet his uncle in the Rainbow department store and shake his hand, proud to pose for a photograph with the voice of Radio Pripyat.

But at home?

At home, it's a different story.

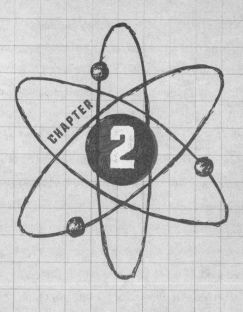

CHAPTER 2

EARLIER THAT EVENING

Yuri's aunt Mayya clears the dinner dishes, scraping the Austrian silver clean of the bounty of pork sausages. Even after several months of living with his aunt and uncle in Pripyat, Yuri can scarcely believe how well they eat. And how full he feels after every meal—uncomfortably so. When he first arrived, Yuri had been shocked to find the grocery stores well stocked with meats, cheese, fresh vegetables—and sweets! Hungarian chocolates, Czechoslovakian licorice, Romanian ice cream . . .

Shortages are routine all over the Soviet Union. The store in Moscow where his own family shops is full of empty shelves. Yuri's mother, along with everyone else, carries an *avoska*—a string "what-if" bag, in case she stumbles upon anything by chance that fills that week's shortage, whether it's canned beets or bathroom cleaner.

In Pripyat, nobody carries an avoska. Aunt Mayya comes home laden with grocery bags. Family dinners are true events, every single night, each one capped off by tasty little *medovik*, or honey cakes.

That's because Pripyat is no backwater town. Pripyat is an *atomgrad*—an atomic city, built to support the great nuclear power plant and financed by the Ministry of Energy. A beautiful dream, a workers' paradise. Families sail little boats up and down the river on Sunday afternoons. The wives of the atomschiki spritz their necks and wrists with European perfume.

Mayya sets the samovar upon the clean table and serves Pavlo and Yuri tea. Yuri glances at his younger cousins, Alina and Lev. He knows what's coming.

"May we listen to the radio?" Alina asks.

Yuri bunches his cloth napkin tightly in his fist, watching the exchange.

"One hour," Pavlo tells his thirteen-year-old daughter. "And be sure to—"

"—keep it low," twelve-year-old Lev finishes his father's sentence.

Pavlo's mouth hints at a smile. He nods. Yuri's cousins scurry from the table to gather around the shortwave radio in the sitting room. A moment later, the faint sounds of the broadcast reach Yuri's ears. He squeezes the napkin tighter.

Pavlo lifts his teacup and blows steam across the surface. Then he takes a dainty sip and sets the cup gently back into the saucer. Even the way the man insists on savoring his tea is decadent, Western, criminal! Yuri has been studying his slight, unassuming uncle in more detail lately. He has decided that everything Pavlo does in the safety of his home is a slap in the face to the State, a private little rebellion.

In the other room, Lev and Alina laugh at something on the radio.

Yuri can't imagine what's so funny about Western propaganda.

He considers the shortwave radio to be the biggest slap of them all. Pavlo permits his children to listen to Radio Liberty, the Western station that everyone knows is funded by the American spies, the CIA, in order to beam outrageous lies into the ears and minds of citizens across the USSR, from Prague to Siberia.

Keep it low, Pavlo tells his children every night. Even in the best Pripyat apartments like his aunt and uncle's, nestled at the top of the finest building at the northern end of grand, poplar-shaded Lenina Prospekt, the walls are thin enough to eavesdrop on one's neighbors.

"You don't approve," Pavlo says, eyeing Yuri across the table.

Yuri has always kept his mouth shut. He is a guest in his uncle's home, after all, boarding free of charge in a spare bedroom for the duration of his internship at the power plant. His sheets are clean, his clothes are washed, his every need met. At sixteen, he lives better than many of the atomschiki, better than many of the plant administrators. He has no right to speak his mind.

The voice of the Radio Liberty announcer drifts in. If Yuri can hear it one room over, then surely their neighbors can, too. And in a city like Pripyat, the eyes and ears of the State are everywhere.

"It makes me a little nervous," Yuri says carefully.

"Hmm," Pavlo says. "I've never taken my Moscow nephew for a nervous sort."

Yuri glances around the dining room. It's really more an alcove, a small space sandwiched between the sitting room—with its lacquered cabinets, shelves full of books passed down as family heirlooms, and deep-red sofa—and the kitchen, where Aunt Mayya hums softly to herself as she dries the dinner dishes. Besides the table and chairs, the only other piece of furniture in the dining room is Pavlo's exercise bike. Fancy indoor exercise equipment—more Western decadence! Yuri had never seen an exercise bike in real life before he arrived at his aunt and uncle's.

Even in an apartment such as this, among the finest in town, the rooms are small, the quarters close. Yuri imagines their neighbors eating their own dinners and listening to the sounds of the illegal radio broadcast coming from the Fomichevs' apartment.

The napkin is a tight cloth ball in Yuri's fist. He clenches his teeth, willing himself to keep his mouth shut. Then Alina begins once again to laugh, and Lev joins in.

"How can you do this?" Yuri blurts out. At the same time, a voice in his head is urging him insistently to shut his mouth. But that voice is drowned out by a red haze that clouds his thoughts.

Uncle Pavlo raises a single bushy eyebrow—a theatrical gesture that Yuri finds infuriating.

"You're the voice of Radio Pripyat!" Yuri says. He knows he should lower his voice, but he can't help himself.

"I am," Pavlo agrees.

"You're a Communist Party member, you go to the meetings, you speak, the people respect you."

Pavlo sips his tea. He dabs at his mustache with a napkin and weighs his words carefully. In the kitchen, ceramic clanks.

"Yuri," Pavlo says, "why are you here, in Pripyat? Why have you worked so hard to secure your internship, and why did you choose Chernobyl?"

"Because I want to be a nuclear engineer," Yuri says easily.

"Ah," Pavlo says. "When I was your age, all I wanted to do was be on the radio. I used to listen to the Radio Yerevan jokes and mimic their voices. My father—your grandfather—bought me a miniature broadcasting set." Pavlo smiles, lost in the memory. "I used to give news reports about the state of our household. What was going to be for dinner. Who won at chess between me and your father."

Yuri wonders what his uncle is getting at. Is this one of those *I see myself in you* kind of speeches he's heard from grownups before? There was that physics teacher at his school in Moscow who always wanted to be a nuclear engineer and had clearly despised teaching . . .

Pavlo seems to be patiently waiting for Yuri to respond. "And so you did it," Yuri says, eventually. "You made the life you wanted while serving the people."

"Mm." His uncle drains his tea, pours another cup from the samovar, and blows steam across the rim. Then he sighs. "Nephew. Do you know what *prisposoblenets* is?"

Yuri frowns at the unfamiliar word.

"Any atomschiki who hope to rise high are prisposoblenets. Any of the Chernobyl administrators who have been there long enough are, too. And Victor Brukhanov—" Yuri starts at the mention of the Chernobyl plant director, the formidable engineer who had raised both the power plant and the city from the muddy banks of the river more than fifteen years ago "—he is perhaps the best one of them all."

"A genius," Yuri guesses. "A man who gets things done."

"In a manner of speaking," Pavlo says. "Some prisposoblenets are geniuses. But not all geniuses are prisposoblenets."

Yuri's eyes drift to the clock on the dining room wall. His shift begins at eleven sharp, and he wants some time alone to gather his thoughts before work. Many of the younger atomschiki stay late, long after their shifts end, to drink endless cups of coffee and watch their colleagues operate the controls, sharing knowledge about new ways to tame the unfathomable atom.

Yuri plans to join their circle, to ease into their conversations, to make himself a part of their group. To do so, he needs to be calm, collected, confident beyond his years. But the way this conversation is going, he'll be rushing to catch the bus to Chernobyl, arriving disheveled and anxious, another dumb kid given a bucket and mop and promptly forgotten about.

His uncle sets his cup in its saucer and again dabs at his mustache. "It means a person who understands without having to be told—instinctively, like an animal—the rules of our Soviet game." Pavlo's eyes sparkle as he surveys his nephew's reaction. Yuri feels scrutinized, not to mention confused.

What Soviet game?

"You mean chess?"

The Soviet Union is justly proud of its chess grand masters, famous the world over for their cunning and skill.

Pavlo lets out a hearty laugh. Startled, Yuri once again bunches up the napkin in his fist.

"Close, nephew. In a manner of speaking, I suppose you're not too far off. Yes—perhaps you're more correct than you know. But in this case, the chessboard is our office buildings, our factories, our broadcast studios,"—he levels a knowing look at Yuri—"our nuclear power plants. And prisposoblenets are both the pawns and the knights, the bishops and the rooks, depending on the situation. They can shape-shift their ideas and the way they talk about them, adapt to the changing whims of Moscow, and they are always able to say what their king would like to hear, to do what their king expects of them, no more and no less. Do you understand?"

Yuri blinks. His uncle seems insistent that Yuri grasp this, eager to impart this knowledge. Yuri suspects that what his uncle speaks of is a form of treason, a rebuke to the State—the secret workings of the Party laid bare.

In the other room, the illegal Radio Liberty broadcast drones on and on.

Yuri's emotions are complicated, and his mind goes as hazy as the river on a dusky afternoon. He feels a surge of something like love for his uncle, for this cozy apartment with its heirloom books and well-stocked pantry, the ringing laughter of his younger cousins. His own father never invites Yuri to linger after dinner at the family's table—he just retreats to the stuffy kitchen to drink vodka and gaze out the window at the snowdrifts that huddle alongside the street like buried giants. Yet the love Yuri feels now, warming his chest, is tempered with cold suspicion. What kind of man speaks this way of the country—the entire *movement*—that granted him the life he'd always dreamed of?

Should his uncle not be grateful for the books and the pantry and the happy family?

At the same time, Yuri knows his uncle is giving shape to the cloudy thoughts that Yuri himself has late at night, mopping corridors and prying rusty nails from steel pipe joints. The way things work, the politics of grown adults, the reason certain things are fixed right away in the power plant while others are left to rot. The reason some engineers rise swiftly in the ranks while others languish.

Yuri forces himself to let go of the napkin and clasps his hands in his lap.

"I understand," he says. Best to simply agree and get this conversation over with, he thinks. He can sort out his thoughts about it later. A sour feeling settles in his stomach.

His uncle frowns. "Are you all right, nephew? Would you like some more tea?" Yuri glances at his untouched cup. The rich amber liquid has stopped steaming. He swallows a lump in his suddenly dry and scratchy throat.

Pavlo smiles sadly. "Perhaps this is too much for an after-dinner chat. I only meant—" He shakes his head. "I know that you're disappointed in the work you're doing at the plant. I know you didn't come here to sweep and mop and fetch coffee. I only wanted to open a door in your mind. Something to remember. The atomschiki on whom you look to model your life, they didn't get to where they are today through hard work and smarts alone. They got there because they are just as good at being prisposoblenets as they are at being atomschiki. They learned to *play the game* and play it well. The earlier you learn this, the better."

Before he knows what is happening, the haze in Yuri's mind sharpens to a cold silver point, a spike that pokes at some buried anger he didn't know he possessed. Everything he can see and hear gathers to drive the spike deeper—the ridiculous exercise bike, the illegal broadcast, the echo of his uncle's stomach-turning words: *They can shape-shift their ideas and the way they talk about them.*

No one has ever spoken of these things to him before, so plainly, so naturally, as if it weren't treason at all. As if it were some everyday conversation about football or the elk his aunt once spotted drinking from the river.

"Yuri?" Pavlo says.

Yuri stands up so quickly, the blood rushes to his head. He barely knows what he's saying as the words tumble out.

"You can't speak of these things!" He wants to scream but has the presence of mind to keep his voice low, and the result is a stage whisper, a bitter hiss. "They don't speak of them in Moscow!"

He flashes to his father staring out at the snowdrifts in the heavy silence of his family's kitchen. Yuri scarcely knows his father—curiously, he can barely remember his face after three months away—but he can confidently say his father isn't a traitor to the State.

Radio Liberty has never been allowed in their house.

Another infuriating smile from his uncle, who says simply, "I assure you, nephew, people talk this way from East Berlin to the Ural Mountains."

Hot tears spring to Yuri's eyes, and he's instantly ashamed but can't seem to gain control of his emotions. There's too much he simply does not understand, but what he *does* understand can be reduced to what comes out next.

"You are turning my cousins into little traitors. Filling their heads with Radio Liberty and—" Yuri pictures Alina and Lev dancing in the living room to blacklisted American music "—*the Talking Heads*—"

"Yuri," his uncle says.

But Yuri can't stop. He's driven by love and worry and anger and frustration all wrapped up together. "At least think of their futures!"

His uncle's flat palm makes a sharp *thwack* as it strikes the lacquered wood of the dining room table. Yuri falls silent. He has never seen Pavlo lose his temper or raise his voice, and he has definitely never seen him smack a table. The cold spike withdraws. All Yuri can do is try to hold his uncle's gaze as the resonant voice of Radio Pripyat hits him.

"That is *all* I think about, nephew. Their futures."

Now Yuri is lost, and more confused than ever. He knows he's spoken out of turn and doesn't dare say anything else, but he can't help but wonder: How is leading his cousins down a path of illegal activities and American propaganda *thinking about their futures*?

His uncle sits back in his chair and glances at his hand as if he regrets letting it act out. Then he exhales softly. "Forgive me."

Pavlo regards Yuri for a long time with an expression Yuri can't read. When he speaks, it's as if the radio voice has left him entirely. "The world is changing," Pavlo says quietly. "I only wish for Alina and Lev to see it as it really is." He pauses. "You too, Yuri."

Yuri feels like the most dull-witted of his classmates back in Moscow. It doesn't make sense: He can identify the parts of a graphite reactor core in his sleep, explain the difference between the three forms of radiation particles—alpha, beta, gamma—but an after-dinner conversation leaves him thoroughly unsettled, with the feeling he's failed to grasp even the most basic truth.

Aunt Mayya enters, bearing a polished silver tray on which sit a dozen generous slices of honey cake.

"Medovik for dessert," she announces, setting the tray upon the table.

"What a treat," Pavlo says, pulling her gently toward him. She gives him a quick peck on the cheek and then swipes her index finger downward so it flicks the tip of his nose.

His aunt and uncle play out this little scene every night, and the warmth of their affection washes over Yuri. He flashes again to his own father, silent at the kitchen window; his mother, staring blearily at the television.

His cousins, drawn by the wafting scent of medovik, rush back into the dining room and take their seats. Yuri remains standing. There is a moment when the entire family's gaze falls upon him, and all Yuri can do is back away from the table.

"Sit down, Yuri," Alina says.

"Stay a while," Lev says.

His cousins have failed to turn off the shortwave and Radio Liberty drones on—something about the war in Afghanistan.

"I have to get ready for work," Yuri mutters. Then he leaves the room.

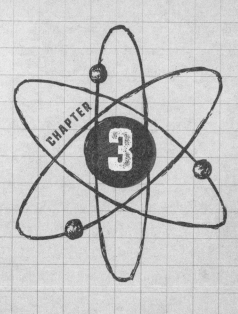

CHAPTER 3

Yuri grips the mop like he's still at his aunt and uncle's table, crushing the cloth napkin in his fist. While the Fomichevs had feasted on Aunt Mayya's medovik, Yuri retreated to the bathroom, splashed cold water on his face, then shut himself away in the spare bedroom.

Now, several hours later, he still can't shake the feeling that he'd behaved like a child throwing a tantrum. The sound of his uncle's palm striking the table echoes in his mind. He feels a rush of despair. For the three months he's been tending to Chernobyl's spills, loose screws, and empty coffeepots, he's felt ill-used and overlooked. He's known all along, inside, that he's more atomschiki than errand boy. What keeps him going is the certainty that one day, others will notice the same thing about him and invite him to linger in the control room, to observe the delicate machinery, to talk into the early morning hours with men twice his age of control rods, graphite, ionization.

But now he's not so sure.

Prisposoblenets. Playing the game.

The floor is spotless, the viscous liquid long since cleaned, yet Yuri continues to attack it with the mop, over and over again in the same spot. What a fool he's been, to think he belongs in the grownup world of the control room, the turbine hall, the catwalks above the reactor core. The engineers are correct to give him a mop, a bucket, a wrench, a hammer. He is lucky they even let him in the building.

Yuri closes his eyes.

One way he's found to soothe dark and lonely thoughts is to let the sounds of the power plant wash over him. From where he stands in the golden corridor, sandwiched between the reactors and the turbine hall, it's easy to imagine he's inside the belly of some great impossible aircraft. The turbines—eight of them arrayed down the length of the hall—hum like jet engines, and Yuri has the peculiar sensation that they are both far away and very close at the same time. If he concentrates, he can feel the vibrations through his work boots, all the way up into his stomach.

Suddenly, the turbines seem to slow. Yuri opens his eyes. *That's odd.* It's as if the jet engine is powering down, and the rapid vibrations—much too fast, ordinarily, for his mind to separate into distinct sounds—slow to a noticeable *woomp woomp woomp woomp.*

He thinks for a moment, narrowing his eyes as if that will help. He vaguely recalls some of the engineers in the sanitary lock discussing a safety test scheduled for tonight. As usual, no one has told him a thing about it.

Yuri can't tell if it's simply the uneasiness he carries with him from earlier in the evening, but his skin crawls with the creeping sense that something has gone very wrong. The Chernobyl-creature is a vast unknowable thing in so many ways, but Yuri has lived among its guts for months, and its shudders, belches, and hums are the soundtrack of his life.

Then, several things happen at once.

Someone opens the door to Control Room 4, and the noise of a heated argument spills out. Yuri can't hear the exact words, but the voices are rising in pitch, approaching hysteria. He turns in time to see two white-clad figures burst from the room and bolt up the hallway toward him.

The walls begin to tremble. Yuri places a palm against the shiny buffed panels to make sure. Yes: It's a ragged shudder, far different than the smooth humming vibrations he's grown used to.

The two men from the control room are closer now, and the alarm on their faces comes into view as the slaps of their work boots reach him.

There's no doubt about it: Something is very wrong. Things begin to happen in rapid succession.

Hysterically, like a taunt, the chorus of Alina's favorite Talking Heads song explodes in his mind.

Run run run run, run run run awaaaaayyyyy . . .

As the two men zip past him without sparing a glance, heading for Control Room 3 (or simply away from Control Room 4), the great Chernobyl-creature begins to moan. It's an unearthly wail, the plaintive cry of some long-imprisoned god rising to the surface of the earth. Except Yuri knows it's not that at all. It's nothing fantastical, nothing out of one of Stanislaw Lem's weird tales—it's actually something far worse.

Steam.

Yuri's mind—the mind that won him this internship in the first place—spins out in horror.

The RBMK reactor is packed with radioactive uranium fuel, cooled by water pumped in from below. When the uranium meets the water, it produces superheated steam, which is directed through the maze of pipes above Yuri's head and into the turbines, where it generates the electricity that races through the Soviet power grid.

To regulate this nuclear chain reaction—and keep everybody in the plant safe—control rods can be raised or lowered into the reactor core. In this way, a delicate balance of energy is achieved.

Normally, it's elegant, even miraculous, the way human beings wring electricity from such dangerous, unstable elements. Yuri is still enchanted by the thought of such cold, precise science at Chernobyl leading to the warm glow of a grandmother's reading lamp 150 kilometers away in Kiev.

Normally, it's beautiful.

But there's nothing normal—or beautiful—about what's happening now.

He should not be able to *hear* the steam. That means there's far too much of it building up instead of being redirected to the turbines. What it *really* means is that the reactor is far too hot. The control rods should have been inserted to break the chain reaction.

But, certainly, the men in Control Room 4 would have done that. It would have been the first safety measure any first-year technician would take, and the room is full of experienced engineers, all of them working together to keep the reactor from running away beyond their control.

Yuri feels the red haze begin to cloud his mind again.

Think, Yuri!

He looks after the two men, but they have vanished—perhaps into

Control Room 3, perhaps into thin air. Ha! Perhaps he dreamed them!

Yuri shakes his head, reins in his wild thoughts. He wills himself to think like an atomschiki.

Stay calm. Focused.

But it's impossible. The steam pressure bellows. Yuri is certain that the problem must be with the *control rods themselves*. A malfunction of some sort. His breath catches in his throat. His mouth goes dry. That would mean—

BANG!

The percussive sound staggers him. He braces himself against the wall. He can't believe this is real. He knows exactly what just happened.

The reactor core is sealed in a concrete vault and capped with a two-thousand-ton concrete-and-steel shield. The weight of such a shield is nearly impossible for Yuri to comprehend. Two thousand Lada automobiles. Two thousand elephants.

And it has just been blown up into the air.

Two thousand tons of concrete and steel, popped like a cork from a bottle of champagne by the power of the superheated steam building up inside the reactor core.

Two thousand cars flung into the air. Two thousand elephants.

The sheer force of it all.

He can't just stand here in the golden corridor like a useless idiot. He tosses his mop aside and runs toward Control Room 4. Golden panels blur together. Up and down the hallway, men are shouting. The lights flicker.

Then Yuri finds that curiously, and very suddenly, his feet have left the floor. For a brief weightless moment, he is running in midair. When the tremendous roar of the explosion comes a split second later, and sound catches up with sight, the world crashes into itself. The polished walls of the golden corridor buckle inward, and Yuri thinks madly of an accordion as they ripple out as far as he can see.

He's thrown completely off his feet. His shoulder slams into the wall, the floor rushes up, and he thrusts an arm in front of his face so that his elbow takes the blow. Pain radiates. Dust chokes his throat. The world comes apart around him.

There are noises he has never heard before and never will again as the Chernobyl-creature tears itself to pieces. Betrayed from within by the invisible atom.

Yuri coughs up blood.

The lights go out.

The time is 1:24.

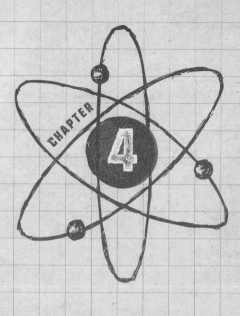

CHAPTER 4

Shimmering light the color of a frozen lake shoots up into the night sky. The glow forms a massive column that seems to vanish into Earth's atmosphere. Ethereal sparks dance around it: sprites of every color, winding ever upward.

Even in her terror, Alina Fomichev finds herself oddly enchanted.

Chernobyl is only two kilometers from her apartment. Exactly forty-three minutes ago—Alina glances at the antique Russian ship's clock, a bulbous timekeeper that had belonged to her grandfather—the Fomichevs had been torn from sleep by a loud thudding *pop* followed by a deep monstrous *BANG*.

War with the Americans! thought Alina as her eyes snapped open in the darkness of her bedroom. But as soon as she joined her brother at the living room window, facing south toward Chernobyl, she changed her mind. The earth wasn't dotted with missile strikes. There were no bombers overhead, no screaming citizens in the streets, no soldiers on patrol. This disaster was local.

And yet what she saw was hardly reassuring.

The nuclear power plant—a hulking beast that had always just been there, looming, without ever seeming to *do* anything—throwing radiant energy straight up from its guts.

Now, as her parents take turns refilling tea from the samovar and talking to friends and neighbors on the telephone, Alina and Lev stand together at the window, watching the column of icy light and its flickering cohort.

A wrapper crinkles. Lev pops a Rot Front candy—a little chocolate cylinder—into his mouth.

"Bear in the north," he announces. All the Rot Front chocolates have funny names.

Lev is always sneaking sweets—toast with butter and sugar, *kartoshka* cakes, extra slices of their mother's medovik. Alina glances at her younger brother. Lev's eager chewing and excited, wide-eyed gaze rubs her the wrong way. He's acting like they're watching this on television, like it's some magnificent special effect unfolding behind the safety of the screen.

"How are you hungry right now?" she says.

"I'm not, dummy. Being hungry has nothing to do with it. I'm savoring the delicious chocolatey flavor of my favorite candy. It's not *filling me up*. I'm not eating a bear in the north because I want to be *full*; I'm eating it because it tastes good. I don't get how you *don't* want one, even though I offered like a trillion times."

"I don't like bear in the north," Alina says. "I like stratosphere."

"There's not really much of a difference," Lev says. "I have a theory—"

"Of course you do."

"—that they just change the names to trick people into thinking they're making different flavors. Someday I'll go to the Rot Front factory to see for myself. Do you think this is aliens?"

Startled, Alina turns to her brother in time to see him unwrap another chocolate. "What?"

"Extraterrestrials. Beings from another galaxy. Big-eyed floaty things with—"

"I know what aliens are."

"—a million tentacles." He waves his arms with squid-like undulations. "I mean that beam of light goes waaaaaaay up there, maybe to the belly of their ship, which could be invisible, because who knows what kind of technology they would have? Better than ours. Better than the Americans."

"Who knows?" Alina says quietly. She glances over her shoulder. Just inside the dining room, her mother and father—both in pajamas—are speaking to each other in hushed tones. Her mother holds the telephone receiver at her side. Her father's slender hand is resting on her shoulder.

"If this is the aliens' first contact with Earth, I wonder why they picked us. Pripyat, I mean. Ukraine. Why not Moscow first, or . . . wait! Maybe they *are* in Moscow, too! And Washington, and—and London, and—"

"Lev!" Alina turns back to her brother.

"Alina!"

He stares at her, unblinking, in the way he knows freaks her out. She feels the itching begin in the back of her mind. Her eyes stray to the ship's clock. She watches the second hand crawl past the black numbers: 5, 10, 15, 20. The even intervals are comforting. They calm the itching.

She folds her arms and stares out the window. The pillar of light shimmers. She feels like she could open the window, extend her arm, and run her hand through the light, as if she were gently grazing stalks of wheat, tickling her palm. Enchantment seeps in and she has to remind herself that she's witnessing something dangerous.

They call the wooded area between Pripyat and Chernobyl the "sanitary zone." Some people have built summer homes there. She thinks of these people now, gazing out their windows in wonder at the looming specter of Chernobyl unleashed.

"Alina," Lev says again. "Alina." Then he lowers his voice to a whisper. *"Alina."*

The itch in her mind blooms into a nagging feeling, as if she's forgotten to do something important. She's always lived with the itch, and it's only ever soothed by little performances like stepping over the cracks in a sidewalk, tapping the four corners of the mirror, closing her bedroom door and opening it three times.

The best remedy of all is listening to American pop music.

But the nagging sensation is more recent—the itch cranked up a notch—and she doesn't yet know how to banish it. She wishes she could put on some music.

"Yuri's in there," she reminds her brother. "He went to work the late shift tonight. This isn't funny."

"I didn't say it was funny, I said what if it was aliens. What if they beamed Yuri up aboard their ship and—"

"It's not a movie, Lev!"

"I know it's not a movie. But maybe it's also not anything bad. Maybe it's *supposed* to happen."

A wrapper crinkles.

"How many of those do you *have*?"

"Thirty-seven."

"And what do you mean *supposed to happen*? Why would they want their power plant to explode? Does *that*"—she points at the pillar of light—"look like something that's *supposed to happen*?"

"Do you know how nuclear power plants work?"

Alina folds her arms. "Do you?"

"Yes." He meets her eyes. "Yuri told me."

"Our cousin told you how nuclear power plants work?"

"A little bit."

"What did he say about two explosions in the middle of the night and a giant beam of light shooting out the top?"

"He didn't get that far. It wasn't a long talk."

Alina closes her eyes. That nagging feeling claws at her mind—*You're forgetting something, this is your fault, you didn't do something you were supposed to do.* She knows, of course, that what is happening at Chernobyl can't possibly be her fault. Something of this magnitude can't possibly be the fault of a thirteen-year-old girl, two kilometers away, in a Pripyat apartment, who forgot to stack the plates in the proper order in the kitchen cabinet, or turn the hot and cold knobs on the sink three times each.

But, as she's come to learn, *knowing* something isn't her fault and getting the nagging feeling to respect that fact are two different things entirely. She makes fists, places them in the pockets of her dressing gown, takes them out, repeats the motion three times. She studies the beam of light across the dark expanse of dense woodland that borders Pripyat. Her careful movements have done nothing to lessen its power. She feels silly—what did she honestly expect, that the energy exploding from Chernobyl would suddenly retract itself, creep sheepishly back inside the reactor like nothing had happened? And yet she can't help it. The urge is impossible to resist, this notion that the way she performs a task is tied, like a sailor's knot, to the grander events of the world.

And to the fate of her family.

"Hey," Lev says gently, recognizing that his sister is in the grip of one of her episodes. "Have one."

He holds up the candy, unwraps it, wraps it back up, unwraps it again, and waits for Alina to nod. Then she takes it, performs the same motions in the same order, and pops it into her mouth. The chocolate is a little too sweet—that's bear in the north for you—but she lets it melt on her tongue and savors it all the same.

"Come on," Lev says, taking her arm. Alina allows herself to be steered over to the Fomichevs' shortwave radio: a top-of-the-line model, better than anything in the electronics section of the Rainbow department store. And much nicer than the boxy *radio tochki* stuck to the wall of every apartment in the city.

Having a father who's the voice of Radio Pripyat has its advantages.

Alina glances over at her father now, clamping the telephone tight against his ear, mouth set in a grim line.

"I have no idea," he says quietly. *"There's been no official statement."* He pauses to choose his words carefully—everybody knows that the KGB, the secret police with agents in every city across the Soviet Union, has the ability to listen to any telephone conversation. *"I assume I will be called in when the Party is ready to inform the people."*

Alina likes to observe her parents when they're only vaguely aware of her presence. Now that she's turned thirteen, she feels like she's crossed an invisible barrier. It's almost possible to think of her parents as *people*, with childhood memories of their own, and lives distinct from the ties that bind them to their children. Tonight her father is simply Pavlo, and she sees that in the way his hand seeks out her mother whenever she walks past, little brushes of affection that relieve some of the pressure from whatever hushed, tense conversation he's having.

She flashes briefly to her father's talk with their cousin Yuri, from Moscow. Sometimes when he speaks to that boy after dinner, the two of them lingering at the table, he becomes a different man entirely from the father she knows.

She turns the volume knob so that it clicks once for ON, then clicks it off before any sound comes out of the speaker. She repeats the motion while Lev watches. Then she clicks it on for real and turns the knob until a low sound comes from the gleaming silver speaker panel.

Carefully, Alina searches the dial for the signal. She navigates fuzz. The State spends millions trying to jam the frequencies of Western broadcasts, and Radio Liberty is sometimes tricky to locate, like a mouse in a field popping out of different holes in its vast warren.

A blazing-fast rock and roll song takes shape, weaving in and out of the radio fuzz. Alina lets the waves of jagged guitars and pounding drums wash over her. Instantly, she feels better. The nagging, clawing feeling retreats to the back of her mind.

"The Clash," she announces dreamily, borne aloft on the relief the music grants her. "They're from England."

"What are they saying?" Lev asks. He hasn't picked up half the English his sister has.

Alina thinks for a moment, translating quickly in her mind. *The ice age is coming, the sun's zooming in, meltdown expected, the wheat's growing thin . . .*

"I don't know," she lies. "It doesn't matter. I just like it."

Her eyes stray to the window. What would it be like to stand underneath the pillar of light, to gaze up at the place where it pierced the veil of the night sky? What would the air smell like? Could she taste the energy on her tongue?

Nuclear power.

The phrase had always given her the shivers. There are so many unknowns buried in those two words. And from the way Yuri speaks about nuclear power to her father, she has her doubts that the scientists themselves understand it completely. So much of it seems unfathomable even to her cousin's brilliant mind.

Once, she overheard Yuri describing Chernobyl to Lev. He spoke of the power plant *as if it were alive*, this massive structure of concrete and steel! As if it were some kind of magnificent unknowable creature.

As the Clash song crashes to a close, her eyes stray once again to the window. What part of the creature is exposed to the night? Its brain? Its heart? Is that shimmering light a geyser of nuclear blood?

The horror of a nuclear creature split open, leaking, *dying* before the eyes of Pripyat, creeps up her spine.

A wrapper crinkles.

Then comes a knock on the apartment door.

And another.

Alina grips her thumb in a tight fist and squeezes. Once. Twice. Three times.

A visitor at this hour, on this night, will not be bringing good news.

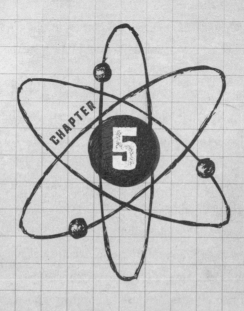

CHAPTER

5

The man at the door is tall and slight, a wisp of a figure in a long leather coat. His thin dark hair is slicked back, and a pair of round-framed spectacles perch high on the bridge of his nose. Underneath his open coat is a jacket and tie, neatly knotted, and a shirt pressed and starched.

A man dressed for a day at the office, in the middle of the night.

His face appears to twitch nervously, though Alina, who has studied this man's face a thousand times at her parents' dinner parties and card games, is fairly certain it never actually *does* twitch. It's like a hummingbird that way—trapped in movements quicker than the eye can catch.

Alina is sure his mind moves the same way—always thrumming,

vibrating with plans, never at rest. She wonders if he ever sleeps.

"Yakiv!" Alina's mother says. She has answered the door, moving more freely than Alina's father, who's still on the telephone, though he's stretched the cord taut into the living room to make his way toward the unexpected visitor.

At Alina's side, her brother freezes in the middle of unwrapping his seventh Rot Front candy. Alina feels the clawing at her mind, calmed by the sounds of the Clash a moment ago, begin to scritch-scratch again.

Here's what she knows about their late-night visitor.

His name is Yakiv Kushnir.

He grew up with her mother in Kiev because their parents were close friends. There's a photograph in black and white of Mayya and Yakiv in a bathtub. Baby Mayya is holding a rubber boat. Baby Yakiv is crying.

They dated as teenagers. Another photograph, a different album on the shelf: Yakiv and Mayya in formal outfits, on the way to a dance, Yakiv affecting an almost American air with an absurd fedora.

They broke up and went their separate ways when Yakiv went to Moscow for university. Here the photographs—some, for the first time, in washed-out, faded color—show only her mother. Until a new boy arrives, that is. A boy named Pavlo, who first shows up in a photograph at a frozen pond, wearing a pair of ice skates. (Her father in ice skates!)

It would be fifteen years after leaving Kiev that Mayya and Yakiv would both end up reunited in Pripyat—each with families of their own.

Alina has heard Yakiv call it *sud'ba*—destiny.

Her father calls it *ne sluchayno*—no accident. Alina understands what her father means by this. Through the years, Yakiv Kushnir has risen through the ranks of the *nomenklatura*—top-level Communist Party positions—to become deputy chairman of the Communist Party of

Pripyat. The second-in-command of nuclear matters in the entire city.

Without being invited, Yakiv steps inside the apartment.

Yakiv can go anywhere he pleases. Get himself appointed to a position of his choosing, anywhere in the Soviet Union. Like, say, the remote atomgrad Pripyat. The same city where his childhood friend and first love, Mayya Fomichev, lives.

This is what her father means by *ne sluchayno*.

"What's he doing here?" Lev whispers.

Alina thinks back to what her father has told Yuri at the dinner table many times: *In matters of great importance, like emergencies, the government will always follow the Party's lead.*

The Soviet Union, ruled by two masters: government and Party.

And what of Yakiv Kushnir, representing the far more powerful Party, the true master, showing up at their home on such a night as this?

"He can do anything he wants," Alina whispers back.

"No," Lev says, "*him*."

A boy of Lev's age follows Yakiv through the Fomichevs' apartment door. Alina takes in his outfit: pressed blue trousers, white shirt tucked in and buttoned up to his neck, around which a bright red kerchief is tied and hangs like a slightly sloppier version of Yakiv's tie.

The uniform of the Young Pioneers, the communist youth group. Nearly everyone at school is a member. As far as Alina knows, this boy is the only one who would bother getting into his full uniform to rush out at two in the morning.

The boy's gaze falls on Alina and Lev, then on the small end table next to them. He stalks over and in one quick motion reaches out and turns off the shortwave radio, silencing Alina's favorite song by the American group the B-52s.

"That's better," the boy says.

The nagging feeling claws at Alina's mind. She fights the urge to turn the radio back on to hear the end of the song. At the same time, she knows she should have turned the shortwave off and put it in its drawer as soon as Yakiv's knock came. But it's all happening so fast.

Out the window, the shimmering pillar glows.

"Hi, Fedir," Lev says to the boy, holding out an upturned palm. "Chocolate?"

Fedir Kushnir, Yakiv's twelve-year-old son, shakes his head. "I'm not hungry."

"It's not about being *hungry*," Lev says, exasperated. "You're just like my sister."

The words give Alina a start. If that were true—if she were anything like Fedir Kushnir—she would crawl into a hole and die.

Lev pops the chocolate into his mouth. "So do you think this is aliens?"

Fedir studies Lev for a moment. "Do I think what is aliens?"

"Um." Lev points out the window, where the light glitters icily.

"Not this again," Alina says.

"What, *that*?" Fedir laughs. "My father says it's a routine safety test."

"See?" Lev nudges his sister. "Routine safety test. It's supposed to happen."

What Alina wants to say, but does not, is this: *Lev, we listen to Radio Liberty every night. We know how different the official explanation and the real truth can be. Why would we believe anything the Kushnirs tell us?*

"Looks pretty safe all right," she mutters. Then she turns away from the two boys as Lev begins to chatter. Her father hangs up the phone and comes into the living room to join her mother and Yakiv Kushnir.

Yakiv smiles at Alina's father. It's usually a nice smile—Yakiv isn't one of the glowering nomenklatura she sees bustling around Pripyat. When he smiles, Alina sees the boy from those black-and-white photos, the boy who took her mother to the dance. And yet now there's something different about that smile. Hints of false good cheer, with tension just beneath.

"Yakiv, my friend," Pavlo greets him. "You're either very early or very late for dinner."

"If Mayya is making her pelmeni, I'll eat those anytime."

"I'm afraid there's only tea," Pavlo says.

There's a pause. Not for the first time, Alina looks at the three grownups and sees them as they were: Yakiv and Mayya dressed for the dance, Mayya and Pavlo caught in blurry color film, whipping around the frozen pond together, arm in arm (she imagines them wobbling, giggling, sliding . . .).

One day she will be a grownup and there will be photos of her at this age to look back on: Alina and Lev dancing by the shortwave and posing awkwardly with cousin Yuri at the table; Alina by the river with her best friend, Sofiya Kozlov, whose father is a nuclear engineer and may well be inside Chernobyl, along with Yuri, right now—

Her father breaks the silence. "What can we do for you, Yakiv? Besides pelmeni."

Yakiv's smile fades. "I take it you've seen the results of the safety test at the plant."

"Safety test!" Alina's mother folds her arms.

"Mmm. *Heard* the results of it, too," Alina's father says. "Pulled us right out of bed. Thought maybe some itchy American trigger finger finally pressed the button."

"Thankfully, no. Just routine. Some kind of disaster simulation. I'm not entirely clear on the scientific details."

"*Simulation*," Alina's mother says. "A *simulation* brought you and Fedir out in the middle of the night for a quick *routine* visit to our house."

"Yes, yes," Yakiv says quickly, dismissing Alina's mother's pointed words with a wave of his hand. His smile reattaches itself. "But I'm *really* here because it occurred to me that your children have never seen Moscow, have they?"

Another pause. Alina's parents seem taken aback by the unlikely question.

"No," Alina chimes in. "We haven't."

"Well," Yakiv says, "Fedir and I are on the way now—always best to get an early start when you've got a long drive ahead of you—and we decided we'd invite you to come with us! What do you say?"

Yakiv looks from Alina's mother, to her father, to Alina, then back to her mother, smiling all the while.

"Moscow," Alina's mother says finally.

"Of course!" Yakiv says. "Springtime is the only way to see the city in all its glory. Red Square. The Kremlin. The Bolshoi." He glances at Alina. "Imagine it!"

Alina feels like she's dreaming. It's almost too perfectly weird: a late-night invitation to a road trip to Moscow, while out the window, Chernobyl hurls some great and horrible energy up into the night sky.

The nagging sensation scratches at her mind. Yakiv's voice is all wrong—as wrong as his smile. She wishes he would open the door and shut it again, three times. Her teeth feel strange. There's something on the tip of her tongue, something that will make her feel better—as good as a song!—if she can only expel it, get it out, out, out—

"You're lying," she says.

Heads swivel. All eyes land on her.

Yakiv lets out a clipped laugh. "I assure you, Alinochka, Moscow is our destination."

Alina blinks. She can't believe what she's just said, but there's no going back now. Even Lev has fallen silent, in the middle of explaining to Fedir how earthworms can regenerate their organs, including their eyes.

"I mean about the routine safety test," Alina clarifies.

Yakiv lets out another clipped laugh. "Alinochka, that's grownup business."

"It's everyone's business," her father says. He folds his arms across his chest. Now both her mother and father are standing with their arms folded identically, staring at Yakiv. A forced chuckle dies in his throat. The grownups stand frozen like this for a moment, and Alina almost bursts out laughing at the absurdity of the scene.

You're dreaming, Alina thinks. *Wake up.*

"Make them come with us, Papa," Fedir says. Then he turns to Lev. "Pack a bag."

Lev doesn't move. All eyes are on Pavlo and Mayya.

As if he's practiced this many times, Yakiv relaxes his face and instantly appears more natural—a trustworthy old friend. Even the hummingbird vibrations she usually detects in his expressions have died away. Now, Yakiv Kushnir is the portrait of reliability, of easy camaraderie, and Alina is astonished that he ever seemed strained and tense in the first place.

Her astonishment grows as he does something she's never seen before.

Yakiv Kushnir reaches out and gently takes her mother's hand away from her hip and grips it in his own. He looks her in the eye and holds his gaze, unblinking.

Now I really must be dreaming, she thinks.

"Please, Mayya," he says softly—as if nobody else is in the room, just

Yakiv and his first love. "For the sake of your family, you must come with us."

There's a moment of stunned silence. Then Alina's father takes a step toward their visitor.

"Look here, Yakiv, that's enough!"

Alina's mother pulls her hand from his grasp.

"No one's going anywhere," her father continues, hints of his Radio Pripyat voice coming through—forceful, persuasive, but never angry, never emotional. It's as if Alina is watching a confrontation in which all three grownups are hiding behind masks. "Not until you tell us exactly what's going on."

"As I said—" Yakiv begins.

Alina's father cuts him off. "No more doublespeak! We're not—"

Alina's mother cuts *him* off. "We're not some potato farmers from the kolkhoz who believe everything you say because you wear a suit and come from the city flashing your Party card around. Remember, I've known you since the days when you wet the bed." She pauses to let that sink in. "Tell us exactly what's going on, and why you're here, Yakiv." She puts her hands on her hips. "Or you can get out."

"You can't talk to my dad that way!" Fedir says, his face the color of borscht.

"Fedir, *hush*," Yakiv hisses at his son. Lev lets out a clipped laugh, then claps a hand over his mouth. Yakiv glances over his shoulder, as if to ensure that the apartment door is really, truly shut. Then he speaks in a low, measured tone.

"It isn't safe in Pripyat. After tonight, it will *never* be safe in Pripyat. You must come with me now—or you will all die."

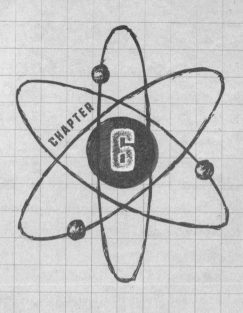

CHAPTER

6

*T*he drum of war thunders and thunders.

Snug in her bed, Sofiya Kozlov comes briefly awake to find a line from her favorite Russian poet, Mayakovsky, floating through her mind. Her eyelids flutter. Shapes emerge from the darkness of her room. As she drifts back to sleep, the words remain.

The drum of war . . .

All at once, Sofiya is aware that she heard a distant *BOOM*—two, in fact, thundering and thundering again. At some point during the night, the sounds invaded her sleeping brain and, like a stone tossed into the Pripyat River, sent Mayakovsky's words rippling through her mind.

The next line of the poem comes and goes. She knows it by heart.

It calls: thrust iron into the living.

She turns over beneath her sheets and hugs her stuffed Cheburashka toy to her chest—the same big-eared, fuzzy creature she's had since she was little and now, at the age of fifteen, isn't quite willing to part with. She lets sleep take her.

Minutes or hours later—it's impossible to tell—Sofiya is shaken awake by a gentle hand upon her shoulder. In the soft glow of her bedside lamp, her father's round, bespectacled face peers down at her. A memory of waking comes to her: thunder and poetry. The feeling that something is off takes hold and sends her bolting upright with a gasp.

"Shhhh." Her father's voice is low and soothing, just as her mother used to soothe her after a nightmare. This new quality settled into him after Sofiya's mother died. She believes it's one of the many ways her father keeps her mother close, adopting bits and pieces of her habits. Sofiya has even heard him singing *"Oh, Moroz, Moroz"* as he putters around the house, sliding papers across the dining room table, getting a light bulb from a high shelf.

"It's okay, Sofiya. It's just me. I'm sorry to wake you."

"Dad." She takes a breath. "What's going on?"

"There's been an incident at the shrub. I have to go to work."

Sofiya rubs her eyes. *The shrub.* Even after all this time, she loves her father for keeping the old joke alive. As a little girl, Sofiya heard that her father worked at *the plant* and drew a picture of him inside the neat rows of hedges and flowers that line Sportyvna Street.

"What kind of incident?"

"There was supposed to be a safety test tonight." Her father is plain-spoken and truthful with her. He promised to always be, as long as she is truthful to him in return. "In case the electricity that feeds the station and keeps it running ever gets cut off, we have to be prepared to maintain power to the coolant pumps before the backup diesel generators can take over—a gap in time of about three minutes. Do you understand what I'm saying so far?"

"You're testing the thing that keeps power going into the plant during a blackout."

"Correct. Good. We call this 'thing' a rundown unit—the idea is that in this three-minute gap of time, we can use the momentum of the winding-down turbines to run the pumps."

"Clever," Sofiya says.

"Er . . . yes." Her father, modest to his core. "Well. Director Brukhanov delayed testing the unit to meet another one of the ministry's impossible schedules, so the test was to finally be performed tonight. And then it wasn't—it seems there was some confusion, orders from Kiev—I don't know the details. Anyway, I returned home when it appeared that the test wasn't going to proceed. But now . . ."

"They did it anyway. Without you there."

"Yes."

"So those booms I thought I maybe dreamt . . ."

"Were real."

"What were they?"

"Explosions."

"At the shrub."

"Yes."

They both go silent. Nothing more needs to be said. Sofiya lets the word sink in: *explosions*. At the nuclear power plant. Where her father is headed.

"Don't go," she says.

Something crosses her father's face—perhaps it's a trick of the dim light, but his features seem to sag with the kind of sorrow Sofiya hasn't seen since the days following her mother's funeral, when they moved around each other in silence through an apartment that no longer felt like home.

"I must go," her father says. "They need me."

Sofiya shakes her head. More words come tumbling through her mind. Words like *meltdown*. The ultimate boogeyman for citizens of Pripyat, all of whom are connected by job or family to the great shrub itself.

"There must be someone else," she says, clinging suddenly to his sleeve.

With what seems like great effort, Hedeon Kozlov places his hand upon Sofiya's, holds it for a moment, then gently removes it. "There is no one else," he says quietly. "Leonid Orlov himself has called me in."

At the mention of Pripyat's all-powerful Communist Party boss, who runs the lives of all the plant personnel with his right-hand man, Yakiv Kushnir, Sofiya nods slowly. They are all beholden to Orlov, from interns like Yuri Fomichev to men of great scientific importance like her father. What else is there for her now but to try to accept the decision? It's not as if a fifteen-year-old girl can stand in the way of Leonid Orlov's will—or in the way of her father's respect for rank. This same respect that drives every grownup she knows in Pripyat (except, perhaps, Pavlo Fomichev at his dinner table).

"Sofiya." Her father hesitates. "I need you to promise me you'll stay put. Don't leave your bedroom. I'll be back as soon as I can."

"What if I have to go to the bathroom?"

"You can do that, of course. I just mean—"

"What if I'm thirsty?"

"Then, of course, yes, you can get a glass of water."

"What if—"

To Sofiya's astonishment, her father leans forward abruptly and kisses her forehead. He has never done this before. She wonders if it's another way he seeks to keep her mother's spirit within him. "Promise me you'll stay put."

He straightens his back. The scent of his aftershave lingers—his one indulgence, an expensive import from Germany. *The best-smelling neck in all of Ukraine,* Sofiya's mother used to tease him.

The memory makes her nod—*Yes, I'll stay put.* She hasn't yet decided what she'll really do, but for now, it's best if she eases her father's mind, like she's done so many times before.

She looks him in the eyes. "I promise," she says.

She holds his gaze as a pang of regret nearly forces her to look away. She thinks of the bargain they've struck, the unspoken agreement that Hedeon Kozlov will never hide anything from his daughter as long as Sofiya acts in the same fashion. As if pure honesty can somehow fill the void left by her mother and grow something new between them, a substitute for her goodness, however makeshift, however desperate. A pact that, lately, she's begun to violate.

Her father knows nothing of her feelings for Yuri Fomichev, for one. And he *definitely* knows nothing of their secret meetings at the railway bridge over Yanov station on the outskirts of town.

"How much do I love you?" her father says.

"As much as the electron loves the atom."

"Correct."

"I love you, too," she says. His hint of a smile lifts his bushy mustache and drops it back down again. Then he leaves her, shutting the bedroom door behind him.

Alone in her room, Sofiya listens to her father's footsteps fade down the corridor of their small apartment. The floorboards creak, then go silent. Sofiya pictures her father standing before the small bureau by the front door, pulling his cap low on his forehead, pocketing his keys, lifting his briefcase, and glancing at himself in the mirror.

The front door opens and closes. Sofiya smiles at how closely she's mapped his behavior.

She waits another minute to make sure her father, in his absentmindedness, hasn't forgotten anything. All is quiet. Without thinking, or weighing it in her mind, Sofiya understands there is no way she is staying put. She leaps forcefully from her bed. As soon as her feet hit the floor, worry quickens her heart.

Yuri is working tonight. Mopping the floors and fetching coffee for the atomschiki in the labyrinth of Chernobyl.

When she first met Yuri over dinner at Alina's apartment, he spoke only of the technical and the scientific, of the important work he was soon to be doing. But at their first midnight rendezvous, Yuri let his guard down. Bitterness crept into his tales of his nights at the power plant. *They barely say a word to me, unless it's "Yuri, something spilled in Control Room Three again."*

He talked of Moscow, too. And of his father's silence. She spoke of her mother's absence.

Her concern for Yuri Fomichev surprises her with its sudden devastating power. She pauses beside her bedside lamp, eyes unfocused and wet, as thoughts of the boy blossom like some great unstoppable garden, too big for its greenhouse.

Then, driven by a purpose she has not yet named, she opens the bedroom door and steps out into the cozy living room—

—which is bathed in an eerie glow. It's as if someone's left a television set on, tuned to late-night static. Except the TV set is most definitely off—there it is, huddled in the corner next to the miniature jungle of her mother's houseplants, which her father tends obsessively. In the weird light, her mother's things are shadowy and unreal. The framed paintings of her native Leningrad, the classical guitar and its stack of sheet music, the little ceramic castles.

Stepping lightly and holding her breath, as if to make a sound would be to alert the glow of her presence, Sofiya tiptoes toward the picture window. Their fifth-floor apartment looks out upon the southern end of Lesi Ukrainki Street. While the source of the glow isn't visible, it has to be Chernobyl, Sofiya thinks. *The shrub.* How, on a night like this, could it possibly be anything else?

She presses her face to the window.

A hundred meters away, a few dozen people are packed together on the railway bridge over Yanov station, Pripyat's main transportation hub. It looks like her neighbors from the apartment blocks decided to have an impromptu party. From the bridge where she has twice met Yuri Fomichev, Sofiya knows there is a fine view of Chernobyl itself. She can see it in her mind's eye, looming across the dark, wooded expanse . . .

What, she wonders, do all these people think is happening? Were they all awakened by the explosions that made only the slightest dent in her own dreams?

As she scans the gathered crowd, bathed in the distant glow, she thinks she sees the familiar shape of her best friend, Alina Fomichev, darting in and out of the throng. Sofiya presses a hand against the glass, wide-eyed and searching. She blinks, and suddenly there's no sign of Alina, nor her brother, Lev, who's always glued to her side. Are Sofiya's eyes playing tricks? Was Alina ever really there at all?

Just like that, her purpose becomes clear.

She will find her friend. At the same time, she will warn her neighbors and make sure they all know the truth.

She will give them her father's message.

A failed safety test.

Explosions.

Once again, Mayakovsky comes and goes:

The earth shivers
hungry
and stripped.

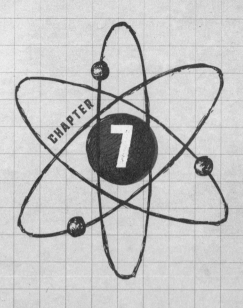

CHAPTER

7

Beyond the dark wood, Chernobyl throws a burning tower of icy blue light into the sky.

Sofiya joins the crowd on the bridge, shouldering between a tall, gray-haired man she recognizes from the apartment block and a young couple sharing a bottle. The sight of the magnificent breach, the energy piercing the darkness, is enough to root her, silent and still, to a spot at the guardrail she can barely see over. For at least a full minute, she stares in awe, forgetting even to look for Alina. The next line from the poem that has lodged in her head like a catchy song writes itself out:

She banishes that one with a quick shake of her head.

The night is chilly, even this deep into spring, and Sofiya can see hints of her breath in the light.

"I built it, you know," the older man says. It takes Sofiya a moment to realize that he's talking to her. "Construction foreman on the first crew to break ground, fifteen years ago now." He gestures back toward the city of Pripyat rising shadowy and silent behind them. "Nothing here but a few huts and dormitories for the workers."

Sofiya glances back, imagines the woodland stretching as far as she could see. No massive apartment blocks, no Raduga Department Store, no playgrounds, no Olympic-size swimming pool. Nature taking back what it had ruled since before there were people on Earth.

Mankind vaporized in a—

She shakes her head.

"It's so beautiful," says the woman to her right, one half of the young couple enjoying their bottle. She sounds entranced, as if she's watching an ice-dancing show.

"Beautiful!" the man to her left exclaims, jostling Sofiya as he turns to face the couple. Then he lowers his voice, as if to let them all in on a secret. "There's nothing beautiful about *American sabotage*."

The other half of the couple, a squat fireplug of a man, shakes his head, smirking. "With all due respect, sir, that's incorrect . . ." He trails off and leans closer to the older man. "I have a friend in the"—he mouths the letters *K G B*—"and he assures me it's the hard-liners in the Kremlin trying to discredit Gorbachev."

The older man straightens up and narrows his eyes. His voice goes cold.

"With all due respect, *sir*, that is preposterous. To say that we Soviets did this to ourselves, after all the sacrifices we've made to get it up and running." He shakes his head sadly. "Your generation is hopeless. You don't build with your hands. You haven't ever had to do a day's honest work in your—"

"It was supposed to be a safety test," Sofiya blurts out. "They call it the rundown unit . . ." Quickly, words pouring out, she relates what her father explained about the three-minute gap in power, the turbines, the coolant pumps. For some reason, even though she is telling these people the truth, her heart is pounding. A sick feeling settles in her stomach. She can tell the older man is skeptical by his deepening scowl.

When she is finished, the man is silent for a moment. The young couple titters and the woman pats her head. "You're adorable," she says. Sofiya ducks away from the woman's hand.

"That's preposterous, little girl," the man says. "Are you saying trained Soviet nuclear engineers don't know how to perform a simple safety test?" He lowers his voice again. "Sabotage," he says. "Mark my words." Then he slides his jacket aside to reveal a holstered pistol. "For when we catch the spies."

Heart hammering against her rib cage, Sofiya backs away. She wonders, briefly, if the man himself is KGB, or at least an informer. It's not like they wear signs around their necks that proclaim SECRET POLICE. It occurs to her that what her father has told her—the truth about the accident—is classified information that hasn't yet been shared with the citizens of Pripyat. And that by sharing it herself, she's breaking the law.

Sofiya moves down the row of people gathered at the guardrail, eyes searching them carefully, but Alina and Lev are nowhere to be seen. There are some smaller children, hoisted onto their parents' shoulders, and a few older teenagers huddled together, but no one she recognizes.

"It's a weapon," says a woman about as old as her mother would be. She speaks with authority, as if she knows exactly what's going on. Sofiya stops to listen. "Look at the outline, the edges of the beam. You can tell it's supposed to be a weapon."

"Everybody knows they've been making weapons there," agrees the man next to her. "It's always been obvious that nuclear power is the best cover for a weapons installation. Look"—he points at the beam, traces it up into the sky—"it's aimed directly at the American spy satellites."

Despite her pounding heart, Sofiya opens her mouth to tell these people the truth, too—and is silenced by a peculiar taste that settles on her tongue. She closes her mouth and the taste remains. It's as if she's licked one of the steel lampposts that line Lenina Prospekt.

"Hey," Sofiya says. A few bystanders turn to her. "Do you taste that in the air?"

The woman with the weapon theory narrows her eyes, sticks out her tongue, and makes a face. "Oh, how peculiar."

"Dull," says a man.

"Rusty," says a teenage girl.

"*Metallic,*" Sofiya says. Murmurs of assent ripple through the crowd. Thoughts of Yuri run through her mind: If the air is corrupted *here*, three kilometers from the shrub, what must it be like inside Chernobyl?

At their second midnight rendezvous, Yuri gave her a gift at this very spot. Now, she pulls the handheld dosimeter from the pocket of her sweatshirt. It's a gray, rectangular object about the size and weight of a telephone receiver, with a screen like a calculator.

I made it for you, he'd said that night, nonchalantly. Sofiya had been amazed. This boy she barely knew had *built* a radiation-measuring device, just like the fire brigades and *militsiya* stationed in Pripyat used.

At the time, when she had recovered her composure, all she could do was laugh nervously. *What am I going to do with it?* she'd asked.

Yuri had seemed a little hurt. He'd only shrugged and gazed off across the dark wood to the shrub.

Afterward, Sofiya realized that he didn't intend for her to *do* anything at all with it—he had simply been using his skills to make her something special, something no other boy could possibly give her.

Either that, or he was just a show-off.

Both, she decided.

Now she presses the little button on the side of the dosimeter. After a moment, a number appears on the calculator screen. Sofiya holds it up, just above her head, to catch the glow from the plant.

2.08

Yuri had told her the number is in the unit of "roentgen per hour," and the acceptably safe dose is minuscule, a tiny fraction—something like 0.3.

This means that Sofiya—and everyone else on the bridge—is being exposed to radiation far beyond normal levels, even three whole kilometers away from the plant.

"What's that you got there?"

It's the old construction foreman, the man with the pistol concealed at his side.

Sofiya hurriedly shoves the dosimeter into her pocket.

"Well?" the man says. "Looks like a neat little gadget. Where'd a girl like you get something like that?" He takes a step toward her.

Before the plan even forms in her mind, Sofiya shouts, "Stop following me!"

The man freezes in place. His eyes shift to the side.

Bystanders turn to regard Sofiya and the man as he puts his hands up. "It's okay," he says. "It's just a mistake."

For a moment, Sofiya wonders if anyone is going to do anything. She can feel the crowd's tension, the questions running through everyone's minds. *Is this man KGB? Should I butt into something that's none of my business?*

Finally, one of the older teenagers breaks the huddle and steps between Sofiya and the man. The boy folds his arms and stares the man down.

"Just a mistake," the man says again. Sofiya thinks she sees a smile tugging at his mouth, but it's hard to tell in the dark. Then the man turns and disappears into the night.

The boy turns to her. "You okay?"

"Yes, thank you," Sofiya says. "Um, you should go back inside."

The boy holds her gaze for a moment, nods once, and rejoins his friends at the guardrail.

"You should all go back inside!" Sofiya calls out. Several bystanders give her their nervous attention. "It's not safe here. The air's not safe."

Nobody moves. Sofiya waits a moment, then turns her back on the gathering and all its murmured wonder. She puts the bridge behind her and heads north, toward the city, to find Alina. No lines of verse come to her, no poetry loops in her mind. Right now, she has no use for pretty words. Right now, she needs her friend.

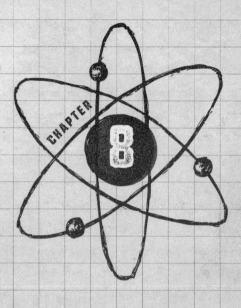

CHAPTER 8

26 APRIL 1986
3:37 A.M.

The UAZ van is an official Pripyat city vehicle: heavy, powerful, built for rugged terrain—and shaped like a loaf of bread. Inside, two rows of benches stretch behind the front seats. Yakiv Kushnir drives and Alina's father sits beside him in the passenger seat, the gearshift a black leather accordion between them. Fedir Kushnir and Lev occupy the middle bench, while Alina sits with her mother in the back.

The van speeds down Lenina Prospekt. Outside, poplars and streetlamps blur past. The sharp smell of petrol comes and goes. Alina has never been inside such an official vehicle before, and feels like she's being taken to Young Pioneers summer camp. Or else being arrested.

A wrapper crinkles. "Last one," Lev announces.

Fedir talks excitedly of Moscow, of touring Red Square, of seeing the great statue of Yuriy Dolgorukiy, founder of the city, up close and in person.

Alina ignores her brother and Fedir. Her left leg bounces on her toes in time with the memory of a song. At her feet is a hastily packed bag—a few changes of clothes, a toothbrush, her cassette player, headphones, and tapes. The clawing at her mind has only grown worse since they abandoned their apartment and followed the Kushnirs down to the vehicle. Except now it's more than a vague, nagging feeling. Now the anxious clawing has a focus, and that focus has a name: Sofiya Kozlov.

To an outsider, their friendship might seem odd. Sofiya is a whole year and a half older than Alina, for starters—so they've never even been classmates.

Alina prefers to stand with her arms folded at the edge of social gather-ings, while Sofiya whirls, mingles, laughs, pops in and out of conversations like a darting minnow.

Alina likes American music; Sofiya prefers Russian poetry and can actu-ally *recite* any number of lengthy poems written by people who are now dead. People with names like Pushkin and Mayakovsky. Just thinking of them conjures up epic boredom for Alina, who will take the Clash or the Talking Heads over a million Pushkins.

Even the way they met was pure chance, the whims of the river on a summer Saturday. The wind had kicked up and blown Sofiya's father's cap all the way to the riverbank, to the Fomichevs' favorite picnic spot, where it landed atop the cooler. The three Kozlovs—Sofiya's mother had still been alive then—had rowed over to retrieve it, laughing, and Alina's father had invited them to join in a toast. While the grownups drank vodka, Sofiya had shared her *plyushka* pastry with Alina and offered up blunt, brutally honest assessments of every teacher at school, and some classmates for good measure.

At first, Alina had been stunned into silence by the older girl's way of speaking. But after an hour together on the banks of the Pripyat, lazing in the sun, Sofiya's honesty and the trust she placed in Alina had made her feel special, welcome, and warm inside.

In return, Alina shared a secret: She told Sofiya about how music soothed the feeling she couldn't name, the nagging in her mind, the sense that she was constantly forgetting something. She had so rarely tried to put the feeling into words before, tears sprang to her eyes as she opened up about it. And Sofiya had listened, and given Alina a hug, and then told her that she would always be there if Alina wanted to talk about what went on in her head.

It had made Alina feel less knotted up inside, and less alone.

Now, Yakiv steers the van past the wide avenue's final apartment blocks. Darkness closes in as they pass the last of the streetlights on the city's southern edge—though that eerie glow still hangs in the night.

That's when the girl on the side of the road catches Alina's eye.

"Stop!" she blurts out.

"No stopping!" Yakiv Kushnir shouts from the driver's seat.

"What is it?" asks Alina's mother.

"That's Sofiya!" Alina jabs a finger into the window, pointing in the direction of the girl—but she's melted into the darkness. And besides, Yakiv is driving way too fast for any one thing to be visible out the window for more than a split second.

"Where?" Alina's mother says.

"She was right there, walking—I know it was her!"

"Alinochka, what would Sofiya be doing out in the streets at this hour? Hedeon would never allow it."

Alina has to stop herself from saying, *Hedeon doesn't always know where she goes at night . . .*

"It was *her*," Alina insists. She leans forward and shouts up to Yakiv. "We have to turn around." The Fomichevs had left in such a hurry, the notion that they should pick up Sofiya to take with them had been distant, unformed, vague. But now she's right here!

"No turning around!" Yakiv says.

Alina feels a combination of shame that she didn't insist on making Yakiv drive to Sofiya's right away, and panic that Sofiya doesn't know how dangerous the situation is. Yakiv's words ring in her head: *You must come with me—or you will all die.*

The warning expands in her mind, until it settles like a low cloud over all of Pripyat. What Yakiv means, she suddenly realizes, is that *anyone left in Pripyat will die.*

Tears spring to Alina's eyes, and the interior of the van hazes into suggestions of her brother, the back of Fedir's head. How could she have been so selfish?

She knows that Sofiya, so much more grown-up, would have thought of Alina instantly, had the situation been reversed.

"Please!" she says. Her mother places a calming hand on her arm.

"We can't stop now," she says gently. "Not for any reason. I'm sorry, Alina. But you must understand—"

"You have to get everyone out!" Alina shouts at Yakiv, who grips the steering wheel tighter and hunches his shoulders. Next to him, her father says something she can't make out and Yakiv responds with some clipped retort. "Not just us!" Alina can't stop herself now. "It's not fair, Yakiv!"

"Your sister's annoying," Fedir says to Lev.

The nagging, clawing feeling builds to a crescendo. She pictures herself smacking the back of Fedir's head. Of course she does not. She clenches her fist instead.

"Alina," her mother says softly. "It's going to be okay. We're together. We're safe."

At the same time, they speed past the bus station and Yakiv takes a sharp left. Three trucks from the Pripyat Fire Brigade come into view out the front windshield, then vanish as Yakiv cranks the steering wheel.

Sirens wail.

Alina swivels her head to stare out the back windshield at the receding city, the apartment blocks dotted with lights. Little pixelated squares, like the computer screen in her classroom. Somewhere out there, Sofiya walks alone—she's sure of it, no matter what her mother says.

Yakiv shifts and the van rumbles as the engine clicks into high gear. The Fomichevs and the Kushnirs speed away east—and soon enough they'll have to strike out toward the north, Alina thinks. Toward Moscow. Out the back window, the sky's icy glow fades into darkness, until even Chernobyl's bright column is taken by the night.

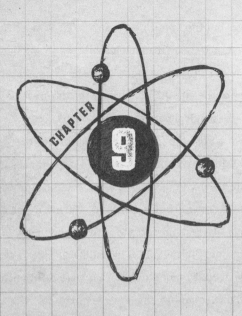

CHAPTER

9

The van's headlights sear two bright dots into the night. Sofiya barely has time to move across the sidewalk, away from the road, before it's practically upon her. She can make out a half dozen figures in its darkened interior, but no more than that.

Militsiya, she thinks.

Yet as the van speeds by, a strange feeling settles over her. She stops walking and stares after it until the feeling passes. Then, shaking her head, she crosses Lenina Prospekt, heading toward the Fomichevs' apartment.

Despite the danger, there's something thrilling about being out in Pripyat when most everyone else is snuggled in their beds. This same feeling crept over her the first time she snuck out to meet Yuri by the train bridge—like she was darting through a secret world she had all to herself. Everything felt more infinite at night, as if she could stumble upon some forgotten corner of the city, hidden during the day, revealed only to those who followed some magical path through the darkness.

Her feet swish across the grassy strip that divides the wide avenues of Lenina Prospekt. In the distance, sirens wail. She glances up at the buildings that loom over the avenue like great toy blocks slammed into the earth by a giant's hand. Several lights blink on. During a normal night, they would be entirely blacked out except for the odd window of an early shift worker or insomniac. But tonight, it looks like the city is starting to wake from its uneasy sleep, as more and more people call their neighbors and spread the word that something has gone very wrong.

At the other end of the avenue, she walks briskly across the sidewalk and into the Fomichevs' building. There is no one in the small lobby. In the empty elevator, she hits the button for the top floor, home to the largest and most luxurious apartments.

Sofiya likes Alina's father, Pavlo Fomichev, but still can't quite shake her first impression.

How strange it is that a radio announcer is given a grander apartment—and can afford finer things, like an exercise bike—than a man like her father, without whom there would be no Chernobyl.

Her father has explained it to her before. Pavlo, for all his bluster around the dinner table—and his flaunting of the Soviet State's rules in the privacy of his home—has shown great skill in being an important Communist Party man in public. Deferential to the right people. Useful to the State.

Meanwhile, Sofiya's father is not even a member of the Party and can only hope to rise so high despite his scientific mind.

The top half of the elevator's rear wall is a mirror. Sofiya studies her face. Her eyes stray to her high forehead—her *mother's* high forehead. They share other features, too, like the untamable curly hair that can only be teased like a pop star's, and eyes the color of a cold winter morning. But it's the forehead in which she sees her mother the most.

The bell dings. The doors open. Sofiya strides quickly down the hall—conscious of her shoes clicking on the linoleum and the lateness of the hour—and stops at the Fomichevs', number 52.

She knocks—three quick raps—and waits a moment. This night, for all its danger, is awash in memory. Sofiya has been here dozens of times, both alone and with her father, awaiting Mayya or Pavlo or Alina throwing open the door, welcoming her inside to the rich smells of Mayya's cooking wafting from the kitchen.

But now she is met with only silence.

She tries again—five raps this time, as hard as she can—and waits. Again: silence.

She takes a deep breath and reaches for the doorknob. It turns. She pushes the door: unlocked! Quickly, furtively, feeling like a burglar, she steps inside and closes the door behind her.

Inside the dark apartment, her eyes are drawn right away to the big, south-facing living room window. Where Sofiya's apartment afforded her a view of the edge of the eerie glow in the sky, the Fomichevs' offers a perfect line of sight to the power plant—an even better view than from the railway bridge. For a moment, she simply stands there in the dark, gazing out at the pillar of light. From here, it looks like it's crackling in the air, charged with the peculiar energy birthed in the belly of the reactor.

Her mouth goes dry as she thinks of Yuri, whose small room, neat as a monk's, is just a few steps away, next to the kitchen.

She fumbles along the wall for the switch and a moment later, the light comes on.

She knows instantly that the apartment is really, truly empty. The living room is in mild disarray, with a pair of jackets tossed across the arm of the sofa, as if someone (Pavlo, judging by the size) couldn't decide which one to take and then simply left them. Teacups are nestled in saucers spread across the coffee table. One of the drawers in the great, impossibly heavy bureau—the one whose glass cases contain the Fomichevs' heirloom books—is wide open.

At the coffee table, Sofiya dips a finger in a half-full teacup. The liquid is slightly warm, maybe room temperature. So she just missed them by a few minutes.

Puzzled, she walks slowly through the rest of the apartment. It would make sense for Pavlo Fomichev, like her own father, to be summoned by the authorities in the middle of a night such as this. But why would he bring Mayya, Alina, and Lev with him to the radio station?

She peeks inside Alina's bedroom. There's the unmade bed, her grandmother's *matryoshka* dolls lined up on her dresser, the reindeer lampshade they both agree is kind of creepy. Here, Sofiya gets an idea. She crosses the room and pulls open the drawer in Alina's small writing desk.

There's an empty space where her portable cassette player and tapes should be.

Alina wouldn't take those if she were just heading out for a few minutes. She packs them for overnight trips, for sleepovers at Sofiya's. And she's taken them now, wherever she's gone.

With growing unease, Sofiya heads back out into the living room. She crosses the plush carpet to stand at the window. Staring out at the glowing pillar, she fights the rising sense that she's been left behind. Yuri and her father are already in the thick of it, and her best friend is nowhere to be found.

Her mother, too: six months gone.

Despite the great danger, she hates feeling like a fly on the wall.

She shoves her hands into the pockets of her sweatshirt, curls her fingers around the hard plastic case of the dosimeter.

Then she has another idea. She heads to the Fomichevs' radio tochki, the yellow box with its single speaker and dial hardwired—like everyone else's—to the living room wall. She clicks it on, expecting to hear Pavlo Fomichev's reassuring voice telling the good people of Pripyat that everything is fine.

Instead, the thick, syrupy strain of some classical symphony fills the room.

Radio Orfey—the official arts and culture station. She clicks over to the news station and finds that *it, too, is playing the same classical symphony.*

She waits a moment for an announcer to break in with a news bulletin. The symphony builds to a crescendo, strings upon strings, a hundred instruments racing one another to the madcap ending.

She turns the radio off before it can get there.

Shakes her head. Tries to think.

Unease turns to dread.

What on Earth is going on?

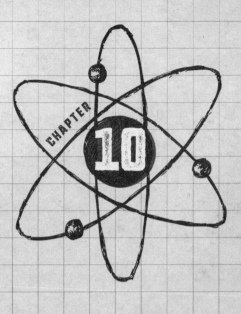

CHAPTER

10

What on Earth is going on?"

Leonid Orlov, head of the Communist Party in Pripyat, fires his question at Sofiya's father, Hedeon Kozlov, practically shouting it across the table where the two of them are seated. Hedeon has been summoned to the Party headquarters, a boxy five-story building with rows of big square windows that form a grid as neat as a chessboard. The building is nicknamed "The White House." It also houses the offices of the Pripyat *ispolkom*—city council—and, on the top floor, the KGB.

Hedeon is aware of the KGB's presence in the building. But in case he was not, the point is driven home by the third man in the room. He's standing in the corner behind Orlov, regarding Hedeon with what could only be called studied disinterest. Unlike Orlov, who looks as if he's been abruptly awakened, dressed himself in the dark, then gulped a pot of coffee in a minute's time, the third man is dressed impeccably, shaved and scrubbed and perfectly calm. Sometimes the man looks elsewhere in the windowless room—the blueprints of Chernobyl tacked up to the wall, or a brown water stain on the ceiling tiles. And yet it always feels like he's holding his gaze directly on Hedeon, without blinking. He wears suspicion like a cloak. It makes the room feel hot, the walls too close together.

Hedeon longs for a glass of cold water, but none is offered. He clears his throat and keeps his voice steady. "I've been in touch with some of my colleagues."

Leonid Orlov is a big man whose bald head perpetually glistens with sweat. As he leans forward to fold his hands and set his elbows on the table, the sleeves of his suit bunch up around his massive arms.

"Well?" he says. "Cut to the chase, Kozlov."

In the corner, the KGB agent adjusts his dark-rimmed glasses.

Under their twin scrutiny, the careful scientific explanation Hedeon has been preparing vanishes from his mind. He pauses, leg bouncing under the table like Sofiya's friend Alina's leg always does. *Where to begin?*

"There was a safety test planned for tonight," he says. "A long overdue test of what we call the 'rundown unit.' You see, in an RBMK reactor like Chernobyl's number four—"

"Yes, yes," Orlov flicks his hand as if shooing a fly. "I've been briefed on all that."

Hedeon blinks. *You have? By whom? And when?* "Oh," he says. The KGB agent regards him placidly. Hedeon is reminded of a lizard sunning itself on a rock in the desert.

"We'll save the *what happened* for the trials, when this is all over," Orlov says. At the word *trials*, Hedeon goes cold. He attempts to swallow and discovers a dry lump in his throat. "Right now, I'm only interested in where we go from here."

"There is one small matter in the *what happened* category to clear up." The voice of the KGB agent is soft, practically a whisper, in contrast to Orlov's constant bluster. Hedeon has to strain to hear the man. The agent levels his gaze at Hedeon. "You were scheduled to oversee the safety test, is that correct?"

In defiance of everything he knows about physics, Hedeon wills himself to shrink to the size of an ant so he can crawl across the floor and conceal himself in a crack in the wall. The agent waits patiently for an answer. Orlov fumbles in the breast pocket of his suit and removes a fat cigar.

"Yes," Hedeon says. He thinks it best to answer the agent with as few words as possible. It's always best to give the KGB very little to work with. The more words you use, the more you try to justify yourself, the more raw material they have for setting their traps.

"And yet you were home, in your apartment, when the test was conducted," the agent says. His soft voice is unwavering.

"Yes," Hedeon says.

The agent waits patiently. Orlov produces a gold lighter, holds the flame to the end of the cigar, and puffs out a cloud that seems to fill half the room. Hedeon's eyes water.

"We received word from Kiev that the plant could not be taken off the grid as planned," Hedeon says. "We knew we would have to wait to conduct the test, but we didn't know for how long. I had been on shift for eighteen hours already, so I left instructions to summon me back as soon as we were given authorization from Kiev that the test could begin. Then I went home."

"I understand that engineers and administrators routinely sleep at the plant," the agent says. "And that there are several cots that can be made available for such a purpose."

Hedeon tries in vain to swallow the dry lump. "That's correct," he says. The smoke from Orlov's cigar catches in his throat. Sweat drips down his spine and pools in the small of his back. He shifts in his seat. "It wasn't just a matter of getting some sleep," Hedeon says. "I have a fifteen-year-old daughter."

"Sofiya," the agent says.

Hedeon finds that he no longer has a voice. He nods.

"Your wife—Sofiya's mother—passed away in November," the agent continues. "The seventh, October Revolution Day."

Hedeon nods again. The agent does not consult a notebook for this information. He simply rattles it off, as if he's memorized it long ago and can recall it at will.

"And so you try not to sleep at the plant, even if it means going home for only an hour or two, because of your obligation to be present for your daughter."

Hedeon tries to find his voice. Orlov and the agent both seem far away, even in the small room, veiled in thick clouds of cigar smoke.

"Yes," he manages at last.

"All right," the agent says. His voice betrays no judgment. Whether or not he approves of Hedeon's conduct, or condemns it, is not apparent.

"Yes," Hedeon says again.

"The *chase*, Kozlov," Orlov reminds him, as if Hedeon has been wasting time idly talking about what he had for supper instead of answering a KGB agent's questions. "We haven't got all night."

"Yes, sir." Hedeon takes a deep breath and finds his voice. "In short, reactor number four no longer exists."

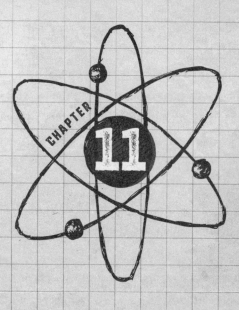

CHAPTER 11

Impossible!" Orlov says. "Utterly impossible. Of course it *exists*. And it's your job to get it up and running."

Hedeon is speechless. The KGB agent scratches his nose, folds his arms, and leans back against the wall. The total and complete impossibility of what Orlov has told him to do threatens to swamp him with despair. *I'm going to prison,* he thinks. *Or else I'm going to be shot.*

His mind flashes to Sofiya, at home in her bed, snuggled with the Cheburashka her mother gave her as a little girl, with its missing eye and matted fur. What will become of her, with her mother gone and her father sent to some Siberian gulag?

"I . . ." Hedeon pauses and begins again. "I'm sorry, but there is no other way to tell you this, sir. It is simply the truth of the matter."

At this, much to Hedeon's astonishment, Orlov begins to laugh. He takes a long puff on his cigar, lets the smoke linger in his mouth, then leans back in his chair and exhales a cloud at the ceiling.

"*The truth of the matter* is that we don't have nuclear accidents in the Soviet Union," Orlov says. "They are unfortunately afflicted with them in America. You have heard of Three Mile Island?"

"Y-yes," Hedeon says at the mention of the famous nuclear reactor melt-down in the American state of Pennsylvania. "But—"

"But we have had a malfunction. And malfunctions can be *fixed*."

Hedeon goes quiet. A strange peace settles over him as the smoke from Orlov's cigar drifts up toward the ceiling in slow, languid curls. He never joined the Party. He has risen as high as he will ever rise in his career. He is likely going to prison anyway—they will no doubt scapegoat him, and several of his colleagues, for this accident. (By throwing others under the bus, Leonid Orlov will wriggle out of blame, of course.)

Now there is nothing left to do but his duty as a scientist: Tell the truth and insist on the proper course of action, even if nothing comes of it. If only he could find a way to warn Sofiya to shelter with the Fomichevs, that it may be a long time before he comes home . . .

If, indeed, he ever comes home at all.

"I didn't summon you here for your doom and gloom, Kozlov," Orlov says. "I need a plan of action from you. How do we get this reactor back to cranking out electricity before I speak to Moscow? I need to tell them it's been dealt with." He checks his silver wristwatch. "I'd like the general sec-retary to wake up to good news."

Hedeon gathers his strength. He straightens his posture and forces his watery eyes to meet Orlov's through the acrid haze.

"Reactor number four hasn't malfunctioned," Hedeon says, surprised at the cold, calculating furor in his voice. "It has *exploded*."

Silence. Hedeon lets the word sink in.

"Nonsense," Orlov says. "I've never heard of a reactor exploding before. You're wasting time, Kozlov."

"No, sir." Hedeon says, shaking his head. "It's *you* that is wasting time. Our instruments measure radiation up to two hundred roentgen per hour, tens of thousands of times beyond what is normal or safe for human beings. And we have already measured that much in the air around the plant. The only reason we don't know how much is because our instruments stop at two hundred. Reactor number four is *open to the sky*. The air. The city." As he speaks of this, one word reverberates through his mind: *Sofiya, Sofiya, Sofiya*.

"Then your instruments are broken!" Orlov shouts.

"They are not, sir!" Hedeon shouts back. His suit is soaked in sweat. The KGB agent regards him implacably, unmoved by his outburst. "You want a plan of action? The only possible plan of action is to evacuate the entire city, as soon as possible. Buses, cars, motorcycles, taxis you can get from Kiev—every citizen must leave. Now. Reactor number four is never coming back online. It's only a matter of time before Pripyat itself becomes completely uninhabitable. And if a new criticality begins—"

"Kozlov!" Orlov tries to interrupt.

Hedeon slams a fist down on the table. It occurs to him even in this moment when he's barely thinking, just speaking as fast as he can, that it's something he's never done before in his life. "If a new criticality begins, if a new explosion damages the other three reactors, then the radiation spread could eventually kill every living and breathing thing on the planet. Chernobyl is no more, sir. Accept it. We must evacuate our people and contain the radiation. That is all we can do, and what we must do."

"Radiation!" roars Orlov. "Radiation!" He points a finger at the side of his head. "The best protection against radiation is *psychological*. Everyone knows that. You are frightened of it, this much is clear—and as a result you have made yourself, in your *weakness*, capable of being hurt by it." Orlov leans forward on his elbows. "But I do not fear radiation—or anything else I cannot see with my own eyes. And in this way I have made myself, in my *strength*, impervious to it." He shakes his head. "*Radiation*."

Hedeon's mouth drops open. He knows that people believe crazy things about radiation. After all, it's as invisible as a ghost, and for many people, about as real. He has heard construction workers doing repair work on the power plant speak of *shitiki,* the contaminated particles in the blood created by radiation.

The way to expel shitiki from your body, according to these men, is to drink vodka.

Hedeon can't really blame them. They don't have the experience of Hedeon and his colleagues, don't deal with radiation and fear its ravages on a daily basis. If you're not a nuclear scientist, what good are words like *alpha, beta, gamma radiation*?

But Leonid Orlov is the head of nuclear matters in Pripyat. To hear him spout such nonsense, as if one of the most dangerous forces that mankind has ever harnessed can be overcome like a brief spell of sadness, has left Hedeon speechless.

What can he hope to accomplish in the face of such ignorance?

The door to the conference room flies open. Hedeon turns to see a bespectacled functionary rush over to Orlov. The aide opens his mouth to speak, then notices the KGB agent in the corner, and gives Orlov a wide-eyed, questioning glance.

"Speak freely," Orlov says. "What is it?"

"Sir . . ." The aide shuffles his feet. "Yakiv Kushnir is gone."

Orlov blinks. "Gone. What do you mean? Gone where?"

Hedeon recognizes the name. He has even met the man once or twice at the Fomichevs' apartment. (He found him nice enough for a high-ranking nomenklatura, if a bit weaselly, with darting eyes and a restless demeanor.) Apparently, this Kushnir grew up with Mayya Fomichev in Kiev and has since worked his way up to being Leonid Orlov's right-hand man in Pripyat.

The aide licks his lips, glances at the KGB agent, then shrugs. "We don't know that yet, sir. It appears he took a city vehicle without authorization and left with his son, sometime in the last few hours."

Leonid Orlov stubs out his cigar on a plate full of crumbs. He closes his eyes, suspending conversation like the haze of smoke that clings to the ceiling. In the moment of silence, *Sofiya, Sofiya, Sofiya* pounds in Hedeon's mind, a hammer against his skull.

Yakiv Kushnir is apparently a deserter, a weasel, a coward, failing to do his duty to the city when its people need him the most—it's true. Yet Hedeon finds that he burns with envy, sharp and bright and sudden. Kushnir might be all those things, but Hedeon has no doubt that he acted in the best interests of his son. And acted swiftly, in defiance of the very system under which Hedeon now squirms.

Kushnir read the writing on the wall, as the Americans say. He read it early and he read it true and he *acted*.

Who, then, is the weasel, really?

For a moment, Hedeon is far from the smoky room and the scrutiny of these men. Far from the city of Pripyat, jamming the gas pedal of a commandeered vehicle down to the floor, tires spitting gravel, speeding down an empty highway, Sofiya beside him, safe and sound.

Could he have done it? Could he have deserted his post and left the people of Pripyat to their fate?

He does not know. Anyway, it doesn't matter now. He is here. He is trapped. He will have to see it through. There is no escaping his fate.

Orlov opens his eyes. He frowns at his aide, seems to ponder something for a moment, then turns to the silent man leaning against the wall with his arms folded across his chest.

"Did you know about this? Did you let him go?"

Fascinated to see a KGB agent confronted like this, Hedeon leans forward in his seat. Orlov is walking a dangerous path but doesn't seem to care.

If the agent is rattled by Orlov's conduct, he keeps it from showing.

"Kushnir will be dealt with," the agent says softly.

Now it's Orlov's turn to strike the table—with the meaty flat of his palm rather than a fist. "I don't want him *dealt with*!" he roars. "I want him found and brought back to me, so I can shoot him myself!" He turns to the aide. "Track him down! And have the militsiya secure every road and bridge around the perimeter of the city. No one else gets out!"

The aide gives a slight bow and scurries from the room.

"Sir, you can't do that!" Hedeon objects. "We have to begin the evacuation!"

Orlov ignores him and bellows, "*Vasiliev!*" The aide reappears in the doorway.

"Anyone else trying to desert their posts will be shot." The aide nods and disappears.

Hedeon's heart sinks. His brain churns, trying to land on some way to help Sofiya escape.

Orlov shakes his head. "*Evacuate.* You'll have me be the first man to lose an entire atomgrad. No. That's ridiculous. Listen to me, Kozlov." Orlov looks at Hedeon with an expression that's almost *pleading*. "Surely this little situation with the reactor can't be *that* bad?"

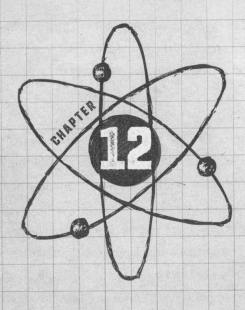

CHAPTER

12

Yuri Fomichev grips the giant metal wheel and tries to turn it clockwise. The wheel does not budge. The strain sends sharp points of agony through his already aching body.

Yuri does not quit. He widens his stance, and the muscles of his shoulders and back tighten up. There are eight of these wheels: the manual controls to open the eight valves that send cooling water into the damaged and dangerously overheated reactor core. These valves are usually operated automatically, but the power is dead, the cables destroyed.

This is the only way.

Yuri closes his eyes. Grits his teeth.

That's when the burned man comes back to him, seared into his mind, etched behind his eyelids. Yuri cries out as a blister on his palm breaks open.

The burned man lives within him now. Forever.

Three hours earlier, Yuri had picked himself up off the floor of the golden corridor. The lights flickered in time with the throbbing of his elbow and ribs. He rubbed his jaw, worked his mouth painfully, praying it wasn't broken.

And then, all at once, there was the man. The first human being to greet Yuri upon his return to the world: more skull than face, more ruined than whole. Dead whether he knew it yet or not.

Skin, scalded red and torn to pieces, hung like tattered curtains from the man's cheekbones, forehead, and chin. He staggered down the golden corridor, holding his ribboned flesh together, just barely, with blistered hands. His voice was a ragged hiss.

Yuri screamed. The man approached, reaching out, eyes bulging from raw meat sockets. Yuri backed against the wall. His body ached. His vision swam. The man imprinted himself into Yuri's mind, half-mad and awakening into horror.

And then the water came and the man was gone. Swept away down the golden corridor as a torrent poured in from the wreckage of the ceiling. Yuri watched him go, flailing, sliding down the hallway like a log in the rapids, heading for a waterfall.

Was the burned man someone he knew?

There was no time to think.

Water swamped Yuri's boots, up to his ankles. He fought the urge to close his eyes, fall to his knees, let the water take him. *Concussion,* he thought.

That would explain the sheer exhaustion, the urge to simply give in.

Instead, he forced himself down the hall he'd mopped every night for three months—now a nightmare version of itself, torn apart by the blast.

The blast.

How could this be happening? What had gone wrong?

He sloshed his way to Control Room 4. The door was gone. Inside, lights were flickering and men were shouting. He saw Anatoly Dyatlov, deputy chief engineer for operations, the man in charge of the control room, screaming at his subordinates. Everyone was covered in fine dust that Yuri figured had sifted down from the ceiling, shaken loose by the blast. The light monitoring the room's radiation level was glowing red. It had always been green before. A strange smell filled the air, like the burned rubber and scorched chrome of a highway pileup. Engineers in white overalls and caps milled about the wall of TV screens, instrument panels, and the 211 glowing dials that represented the control rods.

Yuri noted that all the rods had been inserted into the reactor.

At that moment, two young men in their twenties appeared in the doorway and rushed out of the room, nearly bowling Yuri over.

Yuri knew them both. Leonid Toptunov, an atomschiki he admired, senior reactor control engineer of unit four. Clean-shaven with a slight paunch, Toptunov was both brilliant and kind. He'd once told Yuri that as the child of a senior army officer connected to the space program, he'd had Yuri's namesake—famed cosmonaut Yuri Gagarin—as a babysitter.

The other man was Alexander Akimov, the unit four shift foreman. Well respected and knowledgeable, he had assigned Yuri menial tasks before but had never treated him poorly.

"Yuri!" Toptunov said—he was one of the few nuclear engineers who knew Yuri by name.

What happened? Yuri tried to say, and found that his voice was completely gone. His raspy question was lost in the chaos.

Just outside the doorway to Control Room 4, Toptunov and Akimov braced themselves against the torrent that was rushing past their ankles. Toptunov put a hand on Yuri's shoulder and studied his face.

"Are you all right?" He had to practically shout to be heard.

Yuri's hand went to his forehead, his cheek. Gingerly he pressed a finger against his sore jaw. It came away bloody. So he wasn't just battered, he was cut.

He managed to find his voice. He was determined to be strong in front of the atomschiki.

"The blast knocked me over, but I think I'm okay."

He heard the words come out of his mouth a split second after he'd spoken them. *The blast.* His vision swam again. Toptunov looked into his eyes for a moment. Inside the control room, furious voices rose in argument, crested, died away. Inside his boots, his feet were sopping wet.

"I want to help," Yuri said. "Tell me what I can do."

Toptunov hesitated, glanced at Akimov, then nodded. "We have to get coolant into the reactor by hand. Come with us."

Now the three men have been struggling for hours inside the tiny coolant pipeline compartment. Besides wheels the size of Yuri's entire upper body, the compartment is typical of the Chernobyl-creature's guts: pipes that snake in and out of sight, steel growths with eyes of dials and gauges sprouting from the walls, strange deviations in the poured cement floor. There are no windows, of course.

Yuri has followed the two men deep into the bowels of the creature. On a normal day, he could draw the plant's layout from memory, follow his own inner blueprint. But now, with his head throbbing amidst the chaos, Yuri has lost track of time and space. If Toptunov and Akimov were to leave him here alone, Yuri is not sure that he could find his way out.

While Toptunov and Akimov rest, Yuri takes his turn at the wheel.

He tries to banish the burned man from his mind. But the burned man will not be shoved aside.

He pulls with all his might to turn the wheel. He wills it to move, even a centimeter. The previous four valves took forever to open, but once they got the wheels to budge, the battle was won. But this one is extra stubborn—or else, he thinks darkly, he has simply grown weaker. He cries out as he shreds another blister. Water pours down from the swollen ceiling tiles, soaking him instantly. His hands slip on the wet metal and the momentum and strain send him reeling. Splashing and flailing, he can only hope that when he loses his balance completely, he won't bash his head on a jutting piece of steel.

Suddenly he's enveloped by a pair of strong arms. Bear-hugged, kept upright, then deposited gently on a steel bench attached to the back wall of the chamber.

"Enough, Yuri," Akimov says, letting him go and taking a seat next to him. "Rest with us for a minute."

Mercifully, the compartment is lit by the dim emergency lights that kicked on in the wake of the main power outage following the blast. Yuri glances from Akimov to Toptunov. The water raining down on them has smeared caked grime across their pale faces. Their white overalls have turned the gray of unwashed linens.

Yuri recalls a movie about the Great Patriotic War: Red Army soldiers trapped in a collapsed tunnel, laying mines beneath the German trenches—

A suicide mission.

Yuri shakes his head. "I can get that valve open." He tries to catch his breath. "I'm fine. I don't need to rest."

Toptunov lays a hand on his shoulder. "Yuri, sit."

Yuri tries to shrug him off and finds that he barely has the strength. He meets the engineer's gaze and Toptunov's face splits into two of itself. Then three. Yuri rubs his eyes. "Okay," he agrees. "Maybe just for a minute."

The three of them sit in silence, listening to the symphony of leaks— some small, some large—that are turning the pipeline compartment into a chamber as damp and humid as a Moscow bathhouse.

"What happened back there?" says Yuri. They have all been so focused on wrenching open the valves to supply coolant to the reactor, he hasn't had a moment to ask about the events in the control room that led to the explosion.

"That stubborn fool, Dyatlov, is what happened back there," Akimov says. Then he leans forward and puts his face in his hands and shakes his head.

Even now, when such things seem to matter less than ever, Yuri is shocked to hear disrespect for a superior from a faithful communist like Akimov. He thinks of his uncle Pavlo at the dinner table, telling Yuri of prisposoblenets. It was only last evening, but it feels like a lifetime ago—now that the burned man lives within him.

Toptunov chimes in with a voice that sounds, to Yuri, edged with the frailty of a much older man. The engineer's face splits into its double once again and Yuri struggles to focus.

Something's wrong with me.

"Last night," Toptunov says, "or early this morning, I suppose, was when we were finally scheduled to test the rundown unit."

Yuri notes that the engineer doesn't bother to explain what this is, assuming Yuri already understands, and for this small gesture of respect Yuri is grateful. He decides that once they get out of this, he will ask Toptunov if he can shadow him in the control room sometime.

"We got word from Kiev that reactor four could be taken off the grid," Toptunov continues. "So we began the test at the power level of 720 megawatts."

Akimov lifts his head and takes over the story. "The manual states that the test is never to be run at less than—"

"700 megawatts," Yuri says. He's read the manual.

"Correct, Fomichev," Akimov says. "But what does Dyatlov insist on?"

"200 megawatts," Toptunov says.

Yuri's eyes widen. "But! But that would . . ."

"Make the reactor incredibly, outrageously, stupidly unstable?" Akimov says. "Correct again, Fomichev. I award you a—" Akimov glances around. "I have nothing here to award you."

"We tried to argue," Toptunov says. "I should have insisted. I should have—"

"It's not your fault," Akimov says. "Even if you'd refused, Dyatlov would have found some other poor soul to do it. There's no shortage of men with their eye on your senior reactor control desk."

"So you powered down to 200," Yuri says. Excitement he barely under-stands quickens his heart. Despite everything—the catastrophe, the danger, the dim wet room, his injuries—Yuri has always dreamed of discussing nuclear energy with his atomschiki heroes.

"If only it had stopped at 200," Toptunov says. "I lost control—"

"Leonid," Akimov admonishes.

"It was my fault. We hit 200 and kept decreasing. 100. 75. 50. I couldn't regain control."

"If Dyatlov hadn't ordered it in the first place, you never would have had that problem," Akimov says.

Toptunov frowns. "Power was stalled at 30 megawatts, the absolute minimum. I should have shut it all down and aborted the test right at that moment. But I was a coward. And because of me . . ."

Suddenly, Toptunov leaps to his feet and splashes through the water pooling on the floor of the compartment. With a great heave, he leans over and vomits into the far corner. Then he stands up. "I don't feel so good," he says, weaving his way back to the bench.

I don't either, Yuri thinks. Nausea roils his guts, and he can't get his eyes to focus. For a moment, he drifts far away from this narrow little room, out to the railway bridge with Sofiya Kozlov in the middle of the night . . .

Akimov's voice brings him back to reality, but not all at once.

He feels like he's come down with the flu. And there's a strange metallic taste in his mouth.

"By that point, it was already too late," Akimov says. "The reactor had been poisoned."

"Too much xenon gas," Yuri says. "You'd fallen into negative reactivity."

"Correct," Akimov says. "So when it was actually time to perform the emergency stop for the test, all the control rods were lowered into this poison."

"The power surged," Toptunov says. "There was nothing we could do." He gestures toward the great metal wheels. "The emergency release valves failed. The temperature rose inside the reactor to, I would guess, five thousand degrees centigrade."

"And then," Akimov says.

"Boom," Yuri says quietly.

For a moment, no one speaks. Yuri imagines the force of all that uranium fuel, the graphite-tipped control rods, plus all the radioactive materials in the core, exploding up and out into the air.

"Then we have to keep moving," Yuri says, rising unsteadily to his feet. The room tilts, slides away, then comes back. "We have to get as much coolant in there as possible."

Akimov sighs. "You might as well sit back down, Yuri."

Yuri doesn't understand. "What are you saying? We can't just give up!"

Toptunov points to the ceiling. Water is cascading down. "Where do you think this is coming from?"

It takes a moment for Toptunov's meaning to dawn on Yuri. "Oh," he says. "Oh no."

Somewhere beyond the walls of the compartment, the valves and pipes are completely destroyed. The vital cooling water they've been struggling for hours to release by hand hasn't been flowing into the reactor at all.

It's been draining back down into the compartment itself, onto their heads.

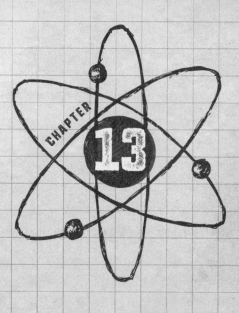

CHAPTER

13

**26 APRIL 1986
5:43 A.M.**

awn breaks gray and heavy over eastern Ukraine. What had been a dark and formless void outside the van lightens to trees, fields, and rolling hills. Springtime bloom is everywhere, and the countryside is lush and green. Alina rubs her eyes. She has not slept but feels like she's stepping from one dream into another. The Talking Heads tape in her cassette player reaches the end of side two and soundtracks the new morning with the jittery sounds of "Road to Nowhere." At her side, her mother dozes.

Her eyes follow a V of soaring geese that dart up suddenly from behind the trees. The beat of the music urges them up, up, up. They shift and swoop as one without breaking formation.

We left Pripyat, she thinks. *We went to bed last night like everything was normal, then we woke up in the middle of the night and left Yuri behind, and Sofiya, and everybody else.*

And now we are here.

She scans the roadside for any sign of where *here* might be. The landscape is no help—it all looks the same, a looping backdrop of trees, fields, rolling hills. Could they be close to the border with Russia? She doesn't know how far that is, exactly. The last time she was in the countryside, her family had stayed with the Kushnirs at Yakiv's dacha, the secluded little vacation home that his rank affords him. The surroundings looked a lot like this. There was a pond, she recalls, a pond with geese . . .

Suddenly, Yakiv steers the van onto the shoulder of the road, then takes a sharp turn onto a gravel pathway that slices through the trees. The vehicle bumps along, jostling everyone inside. Her mother stirs. In the seat in front of her, Lev and Fedir doze as if they're on a peaceful road trip, a long-awaited vacation.

Alina hits STOP on her cassette player and removes her headphones. She shifts in her seat so she can see out the front window. When the van emerges from the woods, she expects to see Yakiv's little dacha, with its peaked awning and porch.

Instead, a dilapidated farmhouse with a sagging roof appears. The whole structure looks to be on the verge of collapse. Some of the wooden siding has rotted away so she can see directly into the dark interior. An old car sits rusting in the yard. Tall weeds sprout from its broken windows and wave lazily in the breeze.

Alina's mother places a gentle hand on her shoulder, the back of her neck.

"Did you sleep, Alinochka?"

Alina shakes her head. "I listened to music."

Her mother forms a crinkly, tired smile. "I dreamed of Kiev. There was a birthday party, with a carousel."

Yakiv hits the brakes and cuts the engine.

"Whose birthday?" Alina says.

Her mother's hand moves to the top of her head, pulls her close. She kisses her forehead. "Yours. But you were older than me."

Alina blinks.

"Here we are," announces Yakiv as he opens his door. Her father does the same and hops out onto the gravel. Stiffly pacing, he walks off the aches of the journey.

Alina's mother releases her. She reaches over the seat back in front of her and wakes her brother. "Time to get up, sleepyhead."

Lev stretches and groans. Next to him, Fedir jolts awake. "Great white shark!" he exclaims.

Alina laughs. "Bad dream?"

Fedir turns in his seat to stare at her. His blank face turns to confusion. He rubs his eyes. Then he comes fully awake, swivels his head from side to side, and regards their surroundings.

"I thought we were going to the dacha," he says.

"So did we," Alina's mother says. Then she taps Alina's knee, which has already begun to bounce with the day's fresh anxieties. "Come."

Alina shoulders her bag and stumbles out onto the gravel. The early morning air is cool and crisp, and she breathes deep. It tastes fresh and clean and she gulps it into her lungs. How different from a morning in Pripyat, with its riot of city smells! Immediately, this darkens her thoughts. What kind of morning greets her friends and neighbors in the city?

Yuri.

Sofiya.

We left them behind.

All around her, unseen birds carry on lively conversations. Something scurries through the underbrush. She turns back the way they came. The highway is entirely hidden by trees.

"This property has recently become available," Yakiv announces when they're all out of the van. "I'm thinking of securing it for a new dacha. What do you think?"

Fedir eyes the decrepit old farmhouse skeptically. "It's not as nice as our other one."

Yakiv laughs—*too loud,* Alina thinks. *Too quickly.* "It's the *land* I'm interested in. We'll build a new dacha, of course."

"Lev," Fedir says, "maybe your family can use our old one when the new one's done."

"Great white shark!" says Lev in return.

There's a weirdness to the morning that strikes Alina as entirely separate from the weirdness of last night. She's like a tuning fork, vibrating with the rhythms of the moment—and Yakiv is coming across all wrong, humming at an odd frequency. She looks to her father, who's regarding Yakiv quietly, thoughtfully. She wills him to fire pointed questions at Yakiv, but he doesn't say anything at all—just takes her mother's hand and pulls her close.

"Well," Yakiv says, the smile plastered to his face, "shall we?" And with that, he leads the way toward the farmhouse's crooked, battered porch. Somewhere nearby, a bird says *wippowooooooo.*

Lev follows his father. "Can I help knock this place down? Can I keep some of the wood? Can we burn it in a bonfire?"

Alina catches up with her parents. "What's going on?" she says. "Why are we here?"

Her father gives her a weary glance. "We're just taking a rest," he says. He holds her gaze for a moment, and she reads something in his eyes. *He knows exactly what's going on,* she thinks. *But he's following along.*

She steps up onto the porch. The wood creaks and groans. Inside, dust floats through beams of light that slice through gaps in the rotten siding. There's a rusty old stove, a wooden table, a few scattered chairs, and not much else. Crooked shelves dangle from the walls. Glass jars and bottles of silty liquid are shoved into a corner, strands of furry cobwebs threading them together.

Yakiv lights an oil lamp and sets it down on the wooden table. The orange glow clashes with the morning light coming in through the walls.

"So!" he clasps his hands in front of him. "Why don't you kids get some sleep? We've still got a long drive ahead of us."

Brandishing the lamp, Yakiv leads Alina, Lev, and Fedir down a narrow hallway that had looked, until they entered it, like a blank space in the wall. The nagging feeling starts to claw at Alina's mind, mercifully distant but gathering steam. She thinks of the headphones and cassette player in her bag. Music is a weapon against it and she gives the bad feeling shape in her mind so she can talk to it. *Better back off. I've got a bag full of music.*

Yakiv pauses in front of a door that looks about to fall from its hinges. But he gives the door a push and it swings open with a creak. He leads them into a small bedroom with four cots made up with sheets and pillows that appear to be much newer—and cleaner—than anything else in the farm-house. *What is this place?* Alina wonders. A musty smell hangs in the air.

"Here you are," Yakiv says.

A thought crosses her mind. "Why are we sleeping during the day and driving at night? Shouldn't it be the other way around?"

Yakiv shoots her a quick, mirthless smile. "Traffic," he says. "Now, pick any bed you like, and get some sleep. We've still got a ways to go."

"I call this one!" Fedir runs over and plops down on a cot in the far corner. A cloud of dust rises and he begins to cough. He waves a hand in front of his face.

Lev observes this, then sits down very carefully on a different cot. Alina picks hers, with sheets and a pillowcase the color of the river on a sunny day (like it was the day she met Sofiya). She sets her bag down beneath it.

"Good night, Dad!" calls Fedir as he crawls beneath the covers. Alina watches the boy curl up happily. *He is really enjoying this trip.*

"Good night, Fedir," Yakiv says. Then he turns to Alina and Lev, nods once, and leaves the room, shutting the door behind him. The room's single window is covered by a curtain fastened to the wall with nails, and the air is thick with gloom.

"Lev," whispers Alina.

"Quiet!" Fedir says. "My dad said we all have to go to sleep."

Alina ignores him. She kneels down next to her brother's cot. "I know that was Sofiya I saw out there on Lenina Prospekt," she says softly.

Lev yawns. "I'm sure she's okay," he whispers back.

Alina's heart quickens. *"Okay?* You heard what Yakiv said. Pripyat's not safe."

"Her dad's a scientist. He'll know how to stay safe. I'm really sleepy, Alina."

"And Yuri? What about him?"

Lev pauses. "I don't know."

The idea forms all at once. She lowers her voice even more and leans toward her brother's ear. *"We have to go back and get them."*

Lev turns over on his cot, showing her the back of his head. "Good night, Alina."

The nagging feeling in her mind explodes into her vision, turning the edges of her sight the color of a fine red mist. She fights the urge to turn her brother over, to make him look at her, to share in her jumpy, jittery feelings. But she manages to leave him be, goes to her own cot, and lies down on top of the sheet. She waits for a while, heart pounding, listening to the blood rush in her head and to Fedir's and Lev's faint, measured breathing. When she's sure both of the boys are asleep, she gets up and creeps out into the hallway. She can hear the voices of her parents and Yakiv, low but audible. She tiptoes to the edge of the main room, keeping to the shadows.

Yakiv and her parents are seated around the table, drinking from dirty glasses. The oil lamp flickers.

"Of *course* we are hiding, Pavlo," Yakiv says. "I know that doesn't sit well with a *loyal communist* like you." His voice drips with sarcasm.

"It's not the hiding I mind," her father says.

"Then what is it that you disapprove of?" Yakiv says. "My son is safe. Your entire family is safe."

"Not Yuri," Alina's mother says.

Yakiv holds up the keys to the van. "Then go back and get him."

Her father crosses his arms over his chest and sighs heavily. Her mother gazes into her cloudy glass. Yakiv smiles and pockets his keys. "I thought so."

"Leonid Orlov will hunt us down," Alina's father says. He sips from his glass, grimaces, and wipes his mouth.

Yakiv's expression darkens. He forgets to keep his voice down and his bitter laughter rattles like tin in Alina's mind. "How about *thank you, Yakiv Kushnir? Thank you* for risking your own life to get me and my entire family away from a deadly catastrophe."

"And straight into another one," Alina's father points out. "Radiation poisoning or a KGB cell isn't much of a choice."

"I see," Yakiv says. "And how would have you preferred me to handle things, Pavlo? File the appropriate documents to take a leave of absence? Humbly request the use of an official van to transport my *good friends* the Fomichevs in? Wait a few weeks for the proper papers to be fixed with the proper stamps?" He takes a long swallow of cloudy liquid. "As soon as I received news of the accident, I could see the immediate future unfold as clearly as if I were watching a film of the next few days. Leonid Orlov, stubborn old apparatchik, desperately trying to appease Moscow while the city chokes on radiation. Refusing to evacuate until everyone's lungs are destroyed. Screaming nonsense about how fear is the true poison. *It's fear that makes you weak, eh, Kushnir?* I've worked with the man for eleven years. I know how he thinks. The city is doomed."

At the word *doomed*, Alina's vision goes misty-red once again. She thinks of Sofiya, alone on the pitch-black street . . .

"We could have warned everyone!" Pavlo protests. "I could have gotten us into the radio station."

"Pavlo," Alina's mother places a calming hand on his forearm.

"I didn't hear you making this noble suggestion when it was time to leave," Yakiv says. "I would have thought that you, of all people, would wholeheartedly approve of sneaking off in the night like criminals. I thought you'd appreciate being able to *act your beliefs*, for once, instead of just carping about them at the dinner table. Tell me, have you given your nephew the prisposoblenets speech yet?"

At this, Alina's father is silent. He turns his head to glare at the cobwebs.

"Just think, Pavlo: You're practically a *dissident* now. One of the heroes that Radio Liberty likes to prop up. Maybe you'll get your own propaganda segment someday."

"That's enough!" Alina's mother says. "Yakiv, we are very grateful for your quick thinking and swift action."

Alina watches a flicker of satisfaction pass across Yakiv's face. A complicated emotion storms inside her. She imagines all the ways that Yakiv must have sought her mother's attention and approval when they were growing up. And the way he does now, it's so . . . *gross*, she thinks. Yet he's not wrong: His swift action could very well have saved all their lives.

What do you call someone who does the right thing for the wrong reasons?

But *was* it the right thing? Because her father isn't wrong, either! Surely they have a responsibility to their fellow citizens to warn them of the danger?

A different path unspools in her mind—one in which her father broadcasts a dire warning from his booth at Radio Pripyat. One in which Yuri and Sofiya join them in their escape.

Instead they're here, stuck in a farmhouse on the verge of collapse, in the middle of nowhere, with Yakiv and Fedir Kushnir.

"So what now?" her mother asks.

"Now?" Yakiv gapes at her. "Now we get some rest. We'll move again at nightfall."

"To *where*, is what Mayya is asking, I believe," her father says wearily.

Yakiv utters that clipped, bitter laugh again. "I didn't exactly have much time to plan."

"So you have no idea."

"I'll think of something."

Alina shrinks back into the shadows of the hallway. *Even Moscow was a lie!*

They abandoned everyone they knew and let Yakiv Kushnir drag them away with no destination in mind. A strange sense of dislocation settles over her. She feels unmoored, set adrift. Far from home, yet no closer to any other place.

Heart pounding, she makes her way back down the hallway. She pauses at the door to the bedroom, which she's left slightly ajar. The musty odor drifts out. Her brother breathes with a faint little whistle, as if he's got a stuffy nose. Her eyes adjust to the deep gloom and she notices, for the first time, that the hallway keeps going, past the bedroom door. Quietly, she makes her way down to the end, where she finds another door. She pushes it gently, no more than a centimeter or two.

Creak.

She looks over her shoulder and waits a moment. Nobody comes to investigate. She pushes the door halfway open. A band of morning light hits her eyes and she blinks away the sudden brightness.

This back room is some kind of small porch, which looks as if it's been used for storage. There are paint cans, rickety shelves full of old tools, a broken lamp, several wooden crates, an old tin sign with a faded red hammer and sickle. The disrepair that's settled over the entire farmhouse is even worse here, and she can see patches of the overgrown backyard through big gaps in the rotten planks. It smells of wet earth and rust. A fat bee flits through the band of light. Her eyes follow it to the farthest corner of the porch—where two old bicycles lean against the wall.

The kernel of an idea forms.

I have to talk to Lev . . .

"You're supposed to be sleeping."

Alina whirls around at the sound of Fedir's voice. The boy is standing in the shadows, hands on his hips, like some Young Pioneers apparition.

Alina pulls the porch door shut with as much nonchalance as she can muster. "Then what are *you* doing up?"

"I have to pee," he says.

"So go."

"Okay," he says, but doesn't move.

"Um," Alina says. "Is there a problem?"

He hesitates. "I don't know where I'm supposed to go. The bathroom doesn't work."

Alina brushes past him on the way to the bedroom. "So find a tree."

She shuts the door behind her and heads straight for her brother's cot. Gently, she shakes him until he's muttering and rubbing his eyes.

"Lev." She glances over her shoulder. Fedir should be gone for another minute or two, at least.

"What is it?" Lev's voice is a croak.

"I know how we can get back to Pripyat. We're going to find Sofiya and Yuri!"

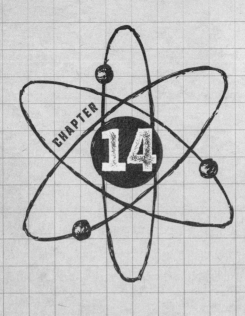

CHAPTER

14

Saturday morning in Pripyat.

If this were a normal Saturday, Sofiya would be getting ready for school.

She has heard that Americans go to school only five days a week, and get Saturdays *and* Sundays off, and can scarcely imagine what she would do with all that glorious free time. But this morning, she's standing at her living room window, watching the bright day swallow up the glow from the shrub.

All that's visible now is the smoke curling up over the edge of the forest, hanging low and dense in the sky.

Mayakovsky comes and goes, curls like that smoke through her mind: *Behold what quiet settles on the world.*

After leaving the Fomichevs' curiously empty apartment, Sofiya made her way back home to wolf down some kasha for breakfast and plot her next move.

She'd tried to warn the people on the railway bridge, but no one had listened.

Now, on the streets below, a curious scene is unfolding. People move about the city as if everything is normal. A row of uniformed children follow their teacher from the Little Goldfish school, like ducklings trailing their mother. Women push baby strollers and gather in the shade of the trees. Nearby, two dogs chase each other in circles, tangling leashes. Men hurry off to work.

At the same time, everything is far from normal. Militsiya vehicles race down the wide avenue. At the edges of the city, soldiers block off roads with heavy wooden barriers manned by armed guards.

Sealing everyone in.

It doesn't make any sense. Sofiya knows for a fact that members of the militsiya and police carry around dosimeters. They are just as capable of measuring the rising radiation in the air as she is. And yet there has been no announcement on the radio, no loudspeakers blaring in the streets—not even a bulletin telling people to stay inside, at the very least.

There's an old joke she has heard Pavlo Fomichev tell: *If you want to fill your fridge with food, plug the fridge into the radio outlet.*

Meaning: Reality is whatever the Party says it is.

If they say there is plenty of food to be had in the shops, then it is so. Never mind the empty shelves, the long lines, the avoska bags.

This explains why everyone below can scurry about on their commutes and morning walks and errands while the militsiya cuts off the city from the outside world.

As she's turning this over in her mind, the phone rings.

Alina! is her first thought. *Yuri!* is her second.

"Hello?" She's practically out of breath as she rushes to grab the receiver from where it hangs on the wall by the radio tochki.

"Sofiya!" Her father's voice. He sounds hushed and garbled, as if he's pressing wool to his mouth.

"Dad! Where are you? Are you okay?"

"Yes. Listen to me very carefully, Sofiya. You must continue to stay inside. Close all the windows. Throw away any food that has been out. And wash everything in the apartment."

Sofiya winces at the word *continue*. Hopefully, her father would never find out that she went to the railway bridge, and to the Fomichevs' apartment. "Okay. Do you know what's happening?"

"I don't have much time, but—reactor number four at the shrub has been completely obliterated."

Sofiya's hand goes to her mouth. *Yuri!*

"I want you to pack a bag. When the buses come, you must get on one. Do you hear me?"

Dazed, Sofiya tries to understand what her father is saying. "Are they evacuating us? To where? For how long? What about—"

"I'm trying," her father says. "That is what I am trying to get them to do. Please—promise me you'll get on a bus."

"Okay, I promise, but what about you?"

"Whether I am with you or not, Sofiya. You must go."

"Why won't you be with me? I can't leave without you."

"You must, if it comes to that. I have a duty." A muffled commotion rises and falls away from somewhere on her father's end of the line. "I have to go now. I love you. Whatever happens, remember that you are always loved. And deserving of the best."

"Dad, no, wait!"

The line goes dead. Numb, Sofiya presses the receiver to her ear, waiting to hear anything at all. On the bureau next to the phone and the radio, behind a glass sliding door, is a row of framed photographs of Sofiya with her mother and father on the banks of the river. Her eyes scan all that remains of sunny afternoons, rowboats and laughter and coolers full of cold drinks and sandwiches. She chokes back a sob but can't do anything to stop the tears from coming.

She has never felt more alone. Her mother, Alina, Yuri, and now her father—all of them completely out of reach. Her mind grasps at stray lines of poetry that flit past like butterflies, but there is nothing to give her any comfort. Only words as empty as the hollow feeling in her chest.

For a moment, the tears are for her alone. For the life she's only just started to create for herself, which now seems out of reach. Since her mother died, she's met a boy, Yuri, who's smarter and more interesting than any of the boys she grew up with. Her friendship with Alina has grown stronger every day. And she has just begun to settle into a new rhythm of life with her father. No longer do they haunt a forlorn apartment. Now they laugh together again.

And it's all been ripped away by a mistake, an accident, some *error* in the turn of a dial, the flip of a switch, an incorrect series of buttons in a control room in the guts of the shrub.

It's not fair.

She hangs up the phone and returns to the window. Pripyat, atomgrad, workers' paradise—a dream of a Soviet city, going about its business, while radiation seeps into its water, its soil, the skin and bones of its people. The very people she sees now, no bigger than ants from up here, but each one a life, each one hopes and dreams and fears and loves.

Sofiya's tears are no longer for her alone. If she is truly loved and deserving of the best, then so are these people, her friends and neighbors.

And if the Party won't tell them what's going on, as they seal them inside the doomed city, then she will double, triple, quadruple her efforts.

She goes to the front-hall closet and rummages around a little box of items her father has brought home, over time, from his lab. She pulls out a *Lepestok*—a cloth mask and respirator with a small filter that covers the mouth. Perhaps now she will be mistaken for one of the officials from the housing bureau who come around to inform residents of new rules and regulations. Or else one of the women from the Komsomol, the Young Communists League.

She glances in the mirror by the door, just like her father does before he leaves the house. Then she checks to make sure the dosimeter is in her pocket and heads out into the empty corridor.

She pauses in front of the neighboring apartment door, rehearsing lines in her head. Then she knocks three times. A moment later a young woman holding a tiny squirming baby against her chest appears. She starts at the sight of the mask.

"Oh! Sofiya. Hello."

"Hello, Nina Davidovich. Please listen to me very carefully. Reactor number four at Chernobyl has been completely destroyed and is leaking radiation into the city. You must close all your windows. Throw away any food that has been out. And wash everything in your apartment . . ."

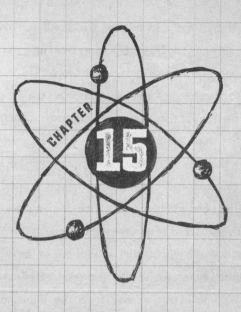

CHAPTER 15

Leonid Orlov swallows his fourth cup of coffee. The conference room is stifling. Over the past few hours, Pripyat's chief Communist Party official has managed to fill the room with more smoke than breathable air. He sets the cup down in its saucer with a *clink* that makes him wince. Lack of sleep is amplifying little sounds, making everything twice as irritating.

He takes a cigar from the box on the table, contemplates it, puts it back. He needs to save his voice for the meeting that will begin as soon as the other Party and city leaders arrive. The mayor, the civil defense chief, Party secretaries from Kiev, Chernobyl plant director Brukhanov, the representative from the KGB (who, much to Orlov's agitation, has yet to sit down, preferring to pace slowly and silently about the room, and lean against the wall). All of them will listen to Hedeon Kozlov's report. Orlov closes his eyes.

He knows exactly how it will play out.

Even in unpredictable circumstances, the Party operators will behave predictably. They will agree with Orlov that the best course of action is not to stoke panic in the city. Then they will accompany Hedeon to the plant itself to inspect the damage, at which point they will all be able to see the emergency crews and firefighters scrambling to contain the problem in an acceptable way. Moscow will again be notified that the situation is under control. Hedeon will protest. The others will silence him. Eventually, an unlucky few—Brukhanov, surely, along with some of the engineers on duty in the control room during the accident—will be arrested, tried, and imprisoned.

One or two will be shot.

These men will be replaced. The city will go about its business. Preparations will continue for the International Workers' Day celebrations on May 1. The people will get their parade. Moscow will be satisfied in the work of Leonid Orlov to manage the incident. He will spend the days following the parade at his dacha in the leafy suburbs of Kiev.

A wave of exhaustion washes over him and he lets himself indulge it. The meeting won't begin for another half hour, at least. He can take a moment for himself.

The sound of the door opening scrapes against his raw nerves. He opens his eyes to see Vasiliev, his assistant, standing across the table with his hands clasped behind his back. Orlov stares at the young man, waiting for his report. Irritation flares. The younger generation can be so *tentative*.

"Well?" Orlov says.

"All roads into the city have been cut off, sir. The only way through is with a special permit. And the long-distance telephone lines have been cut."

"Good. What news of Yakiv Kushnir?"

Vasiliev shuffles his feet and shifts his glance to a place over Orlov's shoulder, where Orlov knows without having to look that the KGB man, whom he knows only as Ivanov, is leaning against the wall, arms folded, surveying the tiny cramped room.

"We have reports that he was spotted heading east out of the city, but we haven't been able to locate him."

"Mmm." Orlov is surprised at his own lack of anger. At first he'd been furious at the news of his closest underling's cowardly defection. But already, the course of things has unfolded in his mind. Kushnir will be found, arrested, tried, shot. What a fool he'd been to try to run in the first place. Moscow will assign Orlov a new second-in-command. Life will go on.

"We will keep searching," Vasiliev adds.

"Let me know as soon as you've located him. I'll want to speak with him myself."

"Of course." Vasiliev doesn't say anything else, but he also doesn't leave the room. Orlov breathes deep to stay calm.

"What else?"

Vasiliev's eyes flick to the KGB agent. "There's a girl, sir." He coughs once into his fist. "We received a call; someone reported her. One of her neighbors. She's going door to door, warning people to stay indoors and wash their food. She knows about the reactor, and she's making noise about a radiation leak in the city."

Another deep breath. How wonderful: a rabble-rouser. Just what he needs troubling his thoughts when he meets with his colleagues from Kiev in—he checks his silver wristwatch—twenty-four minutes.

He thinks for a moment. "How does this girl know what's going on?"

"She's Hedeon Kozlov's daughter."

He opens his mouth to give an order, then thinks better of it. He swivels in his chair. Ivanov's leaning against the wall with his arms folded, that maddeningly placid expression just hanging there on his face.

"Well?" Orlov says. His patience is wearing perilously thin. "Did you hear that?"

Ivanov straightens his posture and smooths his immaculate suit jacket. "Sofiya Kozlov will be dealt with," he says in that soft voice that makes Orlov's skin crawl. "I'll see to it myself." He puts a hand on Orlov's shoulder, and Orlov has to muster all his self-control not to swat it away. He can feel Ivanov's clammy skin through the fabric of his suit. "After this is all over, her father will have to be dealt with, too. As will whoever allowed him the unsupervised freedom to contact his daughter."

Orlov wonders if this is a veiled threat at his handling of the situation. An instant later, he corrects himself: Of *course* it is a threat. But surely he couldn't be expected to remain here, at the nerve center of the operation, and at the same time keep a close eye on the scientist? That's what people like Vasiliev are supposed to be for. Yes. It is Vasiliev who should have locked Hedeon down. And it is Vasiliev who will be held accountable.

"Of course," Orlov says. Then he eyes Vasiliev. "Rotten fruit will be rooted out."

The KGB agent leaves the room without another word. Orlov feels instantly lighter in the man's absence, a weight in his chest lifted. He sits up straight and cracks his knuckles.

"Make sure the ashtrays are clean in meeting room 407," he says. "And fill the water pitchers."

"Yes, sir." Vasiliev exits, and Orlov is alone for the first time since he arrived at the White House, in the middle of the night. He sits for a moment and lets his thoughts unspool outward, toward all the stray pieces scattered across the chessboard.

Sofiya Kozlov, the pawn, rabble-rousing and stoking panic.

Yakiv Kushnir, the knight, deserting his post and betraying his country.

Hedeon Kozlov, the bishop, insisting the reactor can't be fixed.

One by one, he ticks off the ways that each piece will be dealt with. Satisfied that he can wrap everything up to his superiors' satisfaction, Orlov, the king, heads to the bathroom to freshen up for the meeting.

After all, appearances are everything.

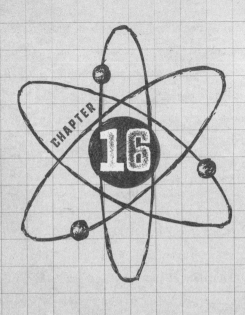

CHAPTER

16

Yuri is alone in the damp, humid darkness. His head throbs, his body aches. No matter how much water he pours down his throat, it stays dry and parched. His sense of time has vanished. Other senses blink in and out like control rod lights on an instrument panel. At times, the sharp tang of scorched metal and burning graphite makes him sick. Other times, he can't smell a thing. The metallic taste in his mouth seems to vanish and reappear without warning. Weird lights strobe at the edges of his vision.

He has thrown up so much, there's nothing left in his stomach. So now he merely retches, heaves, and gags when nausea overtakes him.

On his hands and knees, Yuri wriggles beneath a tangle of sharp-edged rebar and jagged concrete. Before he makes himself as flat as a lizard to crawl into an even smaller, tighter space—nothing more than a tunnel of ruin—he stops to listen. Nothing.

"Sergei Federov!" he calls out to the technician pinned somewhere beneath the rubble. His voice is weak and hoarse. There is no reply.

He will have to keep moving.

Earlier, around sunrise, the ambulances began to evacuate burned and radiation-poisoned men from the plant, close to ninety in all, Akimov and Toptunov among them. Destination: Medical-Sanitary Center Number 126. At the same time, fire crews arrived from local Pripyat stations and from Kiev—186 helmeted firemen in all, their faces shielded behind buglike masks, prowling the wreckage like wraiths from the Great War.

Yuri was sitting in the reserve control room, a relatively unscathed space just off what was left of the golden corridor.

How many hours ago had this begun? He felt numb, his brain dull and his wits duller.

He waited his turn for a medic to assess him and move him to an ambulance so he could join the others at the hospital. It was impossible to keep dark thoughts at bay—from Sofiya's whereabouts to the fate of Uncle Pavlo's family. He hoped against hope the authorities had the good sense to evacuate Pripyat. His uncle's words rang in his head, all those after-dinner chats, his "lessons" on how the Party really operated. But surely, in the face of such grave danger, the nomenklatura would set aside appearances in favor of saving lives?

Just outside the door to the reserve control room, a commotion broke out—voices raised to a near hysterical pitch. Men shouting. Yuri rose from his seat and investigated. A pale, filthy technician he recognized—he was pretty sure the man's name was Vasily—was exhorting two equally filthy firemen, their face shields up.

"You can't just leave Sergei down there! You can't just—"

"He's dead!" shouted one of the exhausted firemen. "The separator drums, the coolant channels—he's buried under all of it now. There's nothing more we can do."

Vasily swayed on his feet and looked as if he were about to collapse. Then he lunged forward and grabbed the fireman by the thick fabric of his protective coat. The second fireman reached in and tried to separate them.

"He's. Not. Dead," Vasily growled. "I heard him screaming!"

The second fireman succeeded in shoving Vasily off his colleague. "We save who we can. We put out the blaze. And we get out of here before this place kills us all. I'm sorry about your friend, but we can't even *fit* down there in all that rubble, much less—"

"Maybe I can fit," Yuri chimed in from the doorway of the reserve control room.

Three heads swiveled. For a moment, nobody spoke. Vasily was breathing hard.

"What's your name?" asked the fireman whom Vasily had accosted.

"Yuri Fomichev."

"Well, Yuri Fomichev, that's a courageous offer. But I'm afraid there's nothing more any of us can do." He looked Yuri up and down. "Come on. We'll get you home."

Yuri shook his head. "I'm waiting for a medic."

The fireman shrugged wearily. "Suit yourself." The two men moved on down the dark corridor, picking their way through fallen pieces of ceiling. Vasily stayed behind.

"I'll search for your friend," Yuri told him.

Vasily shook his head. "I can't ask you to risk your life."

"You didn't ask me. I want to do it." He thought back to the pump room, to the hours spent struggling to open the coolant valves, only to fail so miserably in the end.

He would not leave this place a failure. He would not let the great Chernobyl-beast conquer him with its very death throes.

They were all of them poisoned now, anyway. He tried not to think about what that meant for his future, and focused on making the present moment count for something. Akimov, Toptunov, all the sick, scorched men in the hospital—he would do it for them.

Tears came to Vasily's eyes. He clasped Yuri's hands in his own. "I know he's still alive down there," he said. "Sergei is a fighter. The strongest man I know."

"If he's alive," Yuri said, "I'll find him. Point me in the right direction."

For today, for today, current flows from the RBMK!

The triumphant song drip-drip-drips into Yuri's mind, off-key and echoing strangely. For a queasy moment he's a little boy again, kneeling on the living room floor of his family's Moscow flat, as the world watches the Chernobyl-beast wake for the first time.

And today, and today, the heart of the beast, reactor number four, lies in ruins all around him.

"Almost there," Vasily says, as they clamber over fallen chunks of concrete as big as seaside boulders. Yuri is in good shape—he jogs a few times a week and rows on the Pripyat River, too—but the exertion of the early morning hours with Toptunov and Akimov in the pump room has left him weary. His mouth tastes like he's been eating steel filings. He feels like he's inhabiting an old man's decrepit body. He wishes for a dosimeter, then quickly dismisses the idea.

You don't want to know the radiation level this close to the reactor core.

They descend into a canyon of rubble, and then Yuri stops, frozen in pure astonishment.

"Trotsky's ghost," he whispers.

The roof of the reactor hall is completely gone. Murky, smoky daylight streams in. One of the massive walls has been completely blown apart by the explosion. Anything metal is now twisted and torn and reshaped into a rat's nest of useless pipework. An eerie, vaporous heat corrupts the atmosphere. The great water tanks, the separator drums, the coolant channels he had maintained and polished—all of them have been ripped apart as if by some feral, clawed giant.

Not a giant, Yuri reminds himself. The exact opposite: *microscopic atoms.* Even in his terror, there is wonder at the unimaginable force of it all.

For a moment, Yuri feels as if it's folly to think mankind can ever hope to control such a thing.

"He was up there," Vasily says, pointing at the smoke-filled sky. Yuri knows he means the central hall floor, the steel blocks that once covered the reactor core. "I saw him fall."

Yuri's heart sinks.

The firemen were right. There's no way Sergei is still alive.

His face must have given away his thoughts. Vasily cups his hands around his mouth and yells into the craggy landscape of rubble. Somewhere, a severed cable sparks. Yuri jumps at the sharp *zap!*

"Sergei!" Vasily shouts. Then he stops and holds up a hand. "There!" he says. "You hear?"

Yuri stands perfectly still, listening. At first there's nothing, only the creaks and groans of the beast's guts shifting and moaning. *Vasily is crazy with grief,* he thinks.

Then he hears it: faint but unmistakably human.

"Help! I'm trapped!"

Vasily and Yuri pick their way across broken glass and shredded metal. A jagged edge snags Yuri's forearm and opens up a cut he barely feels. His vision swims in the shimmering heat vapor. They move through the skeletal shadows beneath the destroyed reactor cover.

"In here," Vasily says, indicating a place where debris has fallen to form what looks like the hidden entrance to some fairy-tale cave. Far too narrow for a man of Vasily's stature—or a fireman with protective gear—to enter. *It's going to be a tight squeeze.* Somewhere, a great jet of steam hisses and dies away.

"Okay," Yuri says, blinking away the strobe lights that have begun to trouble his vision.

Vasily grips Yuri's upper arms and looks him in the eyes. "Thank you," he says.

Yuri nods. Then he gets down on his hands and knees and crawls into darkness.

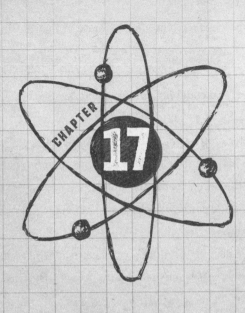

CHAPTER

17

Fedir Kushnir slams a card down on the table: eight of clubs. He flashes his empty hands, wiggles his fingers: *That was my last card.* He grins wolfishly at Lev, seated to his left.

"I can't beat it," Lev says. He picks up Fedir's card and places it with the others in his hand.

"You're the fool *again*!" Fedir says.

Alina, Lev, and Fedir have switched places with their parents, who are getting some sleep in the farmhouse bedroom until it gets dark and they can head out on the road again. This is their ninth hand of durak. Alina and Lev have let Fedir win six of them. If he's happy and pleased with himself,

Alina reasons, he's less likely to stick his nose in their business to disrupt their plan.

"You are a total durak master," Lev says, "and I mean that from the bottom of my heart. You could be a professional. I've never seen anybody so good."

Alina kicks her brother under the table. There's enough sarcasm edging into his voice to make Fedir take notice. But the other boy only nods.

"I know. I'm the best player in the Young Pioneers. When we knock this place down and build our new dacha here, I'm going to have a tournament. You can come watch."

"We would be delighted," Alina says. She sweeps the cards into one big messy pile and begins to stack them neatly. "I could use a little break."

Fedir gets up. "I'm going to the tree."

"Hope everything comes out okay," Lev says. They wait until Fedir goes out the front door.

The nagging feeling claws at Alina's mind. Her heart quickens.

Lev meets her eyes. "Now?"

"Now."

Quickly, quietly, Alina and Lev get up from the table and move down the back hallway. Their parents have left the door open. They pause just before the doorway. Alina listens. Her father and Yakiv Kushnir are snoring. She can't hear her mother's breathing over the men—and her mother tends to be a light sleeper—but it's now or never. She takes two quiet steps past the bedroom, then hurries to the door at the end of the hallway and pulls it open. Lev joins her on the porch and shuts the door carefully behind him. It latches with a faint *click*.

Alina stashed their bags out here earlier, and they shoulder them soundlessly. A mild jolt of comfort settles over her when she feels the corners of her cassette player and her tapes dig into her spine. She scans the porch.

Stripes of dusty sunlight fall across the bicycles.

They cross the grimy floor. Somewhere, bees buzz and mosquitoes whine. Now that she's close to the bikes for the first time, they appear rickety, a patchwork of rust and decay. But what other choice do they have? In a few hours it will be dark, they will be heading east again, and Pripyat will be forever out of reach.

Yuri.

Sofiya.

She walks the bike to the porch's outer door, nudges it open a sliver, and peeks out into the overgrown backyard. The "pee tree," as Lev christened it, is out front, so as long as they cross the backyard and then stick to the woods until they reach the road, they should be safe.

"Good?" Lev whispers. For once, he limits his conversation to a single word. Alina can't remember the last time he didn't stuff at least five sentences into a burst of chatter. Normally, she finds this irritating, but right now she misses it.

She takes one more look at the yard. "Good."

She nudges the door open with her handlebars. The bike bumps once down the single wooden step. A moment later, Lev is beside her. He studies his bike, frowning. In the afternoon light, they look like rusted old antiques, relics of the Great Patriotic War, perhaps. The tires are squishy, but not entirely flat.

Standing just outside the porch, the absurdity of her plan hits her all at once. Last night they drove for several hours—hundreds of kilometers. They are in the middle of nowhere. How could they ever hope to cycle all the way back? She has only been thinking *escape, escape, escape.*

She wants to put her headphones on and lie down and close her eyes.

Nevertheless, she begins to walk her bike through the knee-high grass, heading for the deeper woods. The spokes rip tangled weeds from the earth.

"Where are you going?"

Alina and Lev freeze at the sound of Fedir's voice. Alina turns her head. He's standing in the backyard, half-obscured by weeds, as if sprouting from the ground.

Alina tries to steady her voice. "On a bike ride."

Fedir comes closer. The grass swishes against his Young Pioneers trousers. He puts his hands on his hips. "My father said we all have to stay in the house. We're leaving at dusk."

"Your father's a liar," Alina says. She's surprised at the fierceness of her words. Next to her, Lev laughs in delight.

Fedir's face flushes. "You take that back!" he snarls. "My father can have *your father* thrown in a cell."

"Not anymore," Alina says. "He left without permission. He stole the van from the city. He *deserted his post*."

"He would never do that!" Fedir is practically shrieking. Alina glances at the farmhouse. It's only a dozen or so paces away. Their parents could easily wake to the sound of Fedir's shouting.

"We're not even going to Moscow," Lev adds. Alina has filled him in on the conversation she overheard earlier. "Who knows where we're going? There is no plan. It's all a lie."

Fedir steps forward and gives Lev a hard two-handed shove to the chest. Lev's bicycle trips him up and both bike and boy collapse in the dirt.

The nagging feeling in Alina's mind, her pounding heart, the clawing anxiety that only music can relieve—all of it conspires at once. The sight of Lev sprawled on the ground, Fedir standing over him, speckles the corners of her vision with red mist. Without meaning to, she makes a fist with her right hand and swings her arm at Fedir's head.

Her knuckles connect with his temple. *Thwack.* Her entire arm vibrates. Fedir crumples to the ground.

It's the first punch that Alina Fomichev has ever thrown. Pain blossoms in her wrist and radiates up her arm. For a moment, she's frozen in total shock, surprised by two things at once: that she's actually *struck* Fedir, and how much it hurt to connect her fist with the boy's face.

"Wow," her brother says, bringing her back to reality. He's sitting up in the tall grass. "When did my sister turn into Alexander Yagubkin?"

At the mention of the Soviet Olympic boxing champion, the red mist scatters. Her vision unclouds. Panic sets in.

Fedir isn't moving.

She lets her bike fall to the ground and rushes to his side. He groans and mutters something she can't make out. Then he lies still once again.

"You knocked him out!" Lev says.

Her stomach flips. "I didn't mean to hit him so hard! I've never hit anybody before. I didn't know what I was doing. It was just a reflex!"

Gently, she prods his shoulder. "Fedir! Wake up!" Her heart is racing. The bikes, the journey back to Pripyat, all of it falls away, replaced, in her mind, by the notion that she is terrible—damaged, mean, out of control. The nagging in her mind, the clawing feeling, has urged her toward rage and violence before, but she's always clamped down on it. And now that it's been set free, she's scared that it has grown stronger—too strong for her to resist. She thinks of Sofiya's patience, her advice: *Just breathe.*

Sofiya is bold, yet kind. She doesn't lash out. She is even-tempered. Alina is a coiled spring. Sometimes, she's too wrapped up in her own thoughts to speak. Other times, she's a complete maniac.

Lev is on his feet again. "Let's just *go*," he says.

But Alina doesn't move. She has to know that Fedir is going to be okay, to prove she didn't do something much worse than slugging a boy who hurt her brother.

What if he's dead? What if she killed him?

"Fedir!" She prods him harder, takes him by the shoulder, and gives him a shake.

The side of his face where she hit him is blotchy and red. Drool leaks from his mouth. He begins to stir. His eyes are blank and out of focus. Alina's heart sinks—what if he's brain damaged?

He blinks, sits up—and his eyes focus. His gaze lands on Alina. He scrambles backward. "You punched me in the face!"

Relief washes over her. He sounds like his obnoxious old self.

"Fedir, I'm so sorry. I didn't mean to hit you that hard."

Now that it's obvious Fedir is okay, Lev allows himself to laugh. "Winner, and *still* undefeated, Alina Fomichev!"

Fedir's face scrunches up. Alina watches him fight back tears. She knows what he's going to do before he does it.

"Father!" he shrieks. Then he takes off running toward the farmhouse. Their parents will be awake and outside in half a minute. After this, their parents will never let them out of their sight again.

If they sit here and wait, they might as well say goodbye to Sofiya and Yuri forever.

They won't get another chance.

"Come on!" Alina takes Lev by the sleeve and pulls him toward the edge of the woods. Together, they take off running, weeds whipping their shins.

"What about the bikes?"

"If we go straight to the road, our parents will find us in two seconds. And bikes will just slow us down in the woods."

They hit the tree line together. Thin branches whip back. Leaves tickle her face. There is no trail. Her feet sink down into the loam. Behind them, Fedir's cries fade away.

"Where are we going?" Lev pants beside her.

Her foot crushes something soft and squirmy. She tries not to think about it. "Pripyat," she says.

"How?"

Alina runs silently onward.

I wish I knew.

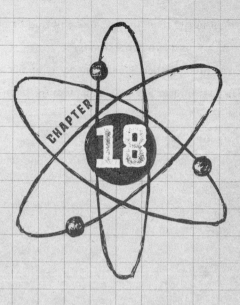

CHAPTER

18

Sofiya is certain that a man is following her.

As soon as she left her apartment building, after delivering her message to whomever would answer the door, Sofiya burst out onto Lesi Ukrainki Street and felt an odd, prickly sensation along the back of her neck.

She chalked it up to the strangeness of the afternoon. If the city's atmosphere had struck her as odd from her apartment window, down on the street it was positively eerie. People rushed to and from the shops, laden with groceries for the May Day celebrations. Meanwhile, the militsiya had blocked off the southern end of Lenina Prospekt. And presiding over all of it is the dull, gritty sky.

But the prickly sensation only grows as she visits building after building. Knocking on doors, giving people the truth that the radio won't.

It isn't until she works her way north, then east on Kurchatov Street, that she spots the man for the first time—and realizes with horror that it isn't the first time at all, that she's been catching glimpses of him all afternoon.

Across the street in a shop window's reflection.

Reading a newspaper on a bench.

Stooping to pet someone's fluffy black terrier.

It's not the man from the railway bridge, of that much she's certain. This man is younger and well dressed and—what's the word she's looking for?—*forgettable*. Nothing about him makes him stand out. Even his dark-rimmed glasses, which might be stylish on someone else, simply blend into his bland features.

He must be KGB.

She thinks of her father's words: *Whether I am with you or not, Sofiya.*

Has he been arrested? Is he all alone in a cell? Has he been *shot*?

Her nerves jangle as she enters the lobby of an apartment block. She thinks of all the times she tried to comfort Alina, giving her hugs and watching helplessly as Alina withdrew into herself while her legs bounced and she worked her mouth, chewing her lip till it bled.

It claws my mind, Alina had explained. *It makes me feel like I'm always forgetting something.*

Now, Sofiya glances back over her shoulder as she waits for the elevator. The man is nowhere to be seen. Still, she is beginning to better understand how Alina's mind works. It's like a sickly, burbling fear. A numbness beneath the skin, all the way down to the fingers and toes.

The elevator never comes. Sofiya jabs the button again, then turns and takes in the lobby: lime-colored walls, a single bench upon which someone's left a sock, a bulletin board full of tacked-up rules and regulations. She watches the street outside through the glass of the front door. Still no sign of the man.

While she waits, she checks her dosimeter. 3.08. The radiation level has been rising steadily throughout the day.

She wishes that instead of telling people to *stay inside*, she could tell them to *get out of the city*.

She wishes *she* could get out of the city. Sofiya, her father, Yuri, Alina—all of them together, all of them safe.

But she can't go anywhere. Nobody can leave. The militsiya have seen to that.

She jabs the button one last time and listens for the hum of the elevator. Silence. It must be broken. No surprise there—the elevator in her own building works only about half the time. She takes the stairs. The narrow stairwell smells of mildew. She comes to a small landing, turns the corner—

—and bumps right into Forgettable Man. He's leaning casually against the wall, examining his fingernails.

She turns to run, expecting to feel the iron grip of the KGB on her arm, yanking her backward, flinging her up against the wall.

Instead, a soft voice says, "Stop, please."

For reasons beyond her comprehension, she does just that.

The voice in her head screams *RUN RUN RUN*. Yet she stays put on the landing. It's as if the man's voice has slithered into her mind and flipped a switch to paste her feet to the linoleum floor.

There are stories of KGB mind control. Human experiments. Telepathy.

Maybe they're not stories.

Sofiya turns to face the man. The world feels like it's moving in slow motion. He swipes a finger to remove a speck of food from the side of his mouth. Sofiya has the impression that he has been having a snack while he waits for her.

How did he get here ahead of me? Did he disable the elevator himself?

"You've been busy," he says. He doesn't sound angry or threatening. He sounds like he's stating a fact.

What do you say to the KGB? Sofiya doesn't know.

"Soon the world won't have a rib intact," she blurts out.

"And its soul will be pulled out," Forgettable Man says in return. "Tell me, Sofiya, is it your father who reads Mayakovsky to you? Or is it Yuri Fomichev?"

Your father. Yuri Fomichev. Forgettable Man doesn't put any particular intonation into those words, but hearing them in his soft voice raises goose bumps on Sofiya's arms. A world of meaning, of threats and implications.

"Neither," she says. "I read it myself."

"A true revolutionary," he says. "But it's Yuri Fomichev who made you the dosimeter you're carrying in your pocket."

She tries to meet his eyes and finds nothing there, just two black pools devoid of expression. She looks away.

"May I see it?" he says.

How can he know this? Sofiya thinks of all the doors she's knocked on, dozens upon dozens of her neighbors, some of whom surely saw the dosimeter.

And one—or more—of them picked up the phone to report me.

The voice in her head no longer urges her to run. It doesn't say anything at all. Numb, she reaches into her pocket and removes the device. She holds it out to Forgettable Man. His hand is as clammy as a fish. He studies the dosimeter. Then he presses the button to get a reading: 3.09.

"Ah," he says. "This is faulty. Broken. Incorrect." He pockets the device.

"You've been stoking panic based on false information."

Again, Sofiya is silent. What is she expected to say to this? It's like Pavlo Fomichev's stupid joke all over again: *If you want to fill your fridge with food, plug the fridge into the radio outlet.*

Reality is what we say it is.

Forgettable Man regards her inscrutably. He makes no attempt to detain her, or to end their conversation. He simply stands there. Sofiya finds this incredibly disconcerting.

"Yuri Fomichev is still inside the plant," the man says. "The small accident is being contained, and we are working to make sure all the plant personnel get out safely. Whether or not Yuri is among them depends on how much trouble you're going to make."

Sofiya's mouth goes dry. *RUN RUN RUN RUN* says the voice in her head.

"People do get lost," he says. "It happens all the time."

Forgettable Man walks past her. His shoes click-clack on the landing, then he is gone. A hint of smoke lingers in his wake.

Her mind races. *Yuri's still inside the plant . . .*

But what about my father?

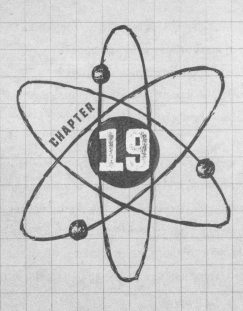

CHAPTER 19

Hedeon Kozlov clamps a hand on his hat as he runs in a low crouch away from the helicopter. The rotor wash is a deafening gale, a hurricane wind. He looks back to see more figures, shaded gray and formless in the dusk, spew from the helicopter door and drop into the same low jog away from the churning machine. He makes out the shapes of Leonid Orlov and his nervous assistant, Vasiliev—both of them, like Hedeon, clad in the bulky protective gear worn by firefighters and militsiya. The other two men are Communist Party officials flown in from Kiev. He was introduced to them in the chopper but did not retain their names or positions.

These men are all the same.

None of them are scientists. Researchers. Atomschiki.

They are functionaries, nomenklatura, apparatchiks.

They are not here to validate Hedeon's opinions.

They are here to play games, jockey for position, ensure that everything Moscow hears about the accident is precisely tuned to minimize the damage to their careers.

Hedeon outpaces the rotor wash. The hurricane winds die away. Behind him, the chopper lifts off, and he can't help but watch as it becomes a dark beetle dangling from the darkening sky, then vanishes over the forest.

Before the government officials can overtake him, Hedeon moves across the landing field, past the huge, eerily placid pools of the coolant reservoirs, toward the turbine hall and, just beyond it, reactor number four.

Or what's left of it.

Now, as dusk creeps across Ukraine, the bright pillar that had been disguised by daylight is coming back into view. The light spears the sky. He can imagine how some might be awestruck at its strange beauty, but Hedeon sees only destruction in its icy emanations.

Alpha, beta, gamma particles.

High-energy radiation.

Unstable atoms, disintegrating before his eyes.

Shooting through people like a swarm of microscopic wasps, deadly stingers at the ready, changing them, corrupting them down to their own atomic cores, scrambling their cells.

He has not been given a dosimeter, but his mind calculates the likely roentgen per hour of the naked radiation, exposed to the air for an entire day, this close to the reactor core. A deadly number beyond imagining.

He takes note of the metallic taste of the air, the burning-chrome odor. He notes how easily this taste, this smell, seeps through his mask and face shield.

The flat expanse between the reservoirs and the reactor is littered with the power plant's guts. Teams of firemen mill about like cosmonauts on the moon, oddly weightless in their bulky suits, picking up chunks of graphite with their gloved hands.

Someone claps him on the back. Hedeon turns to find Orlov standing beside him.

The man has taken off his mask and face shield. He breathes deeply. "Small price to pay for correcting the mistakes of nature," he says.

Hedeon is speechless. It's an oddly philosophical statement from Leonid Orlov. Then he recalls the meaning of the well-worn Soviet phrase—*correcting the mistakes of nature*, meaning: These gargantuan reactors are the beginning of a new era of Soviet power. Nuclear energy can be used for anything. To destroy entire mountain ranges, reshape oceans, carve out new canyons, if that is the will of the State.

"You should be wearing a mask at the very least, sir!" Hedeon says.

"Nonsense." Orlov brandishes a flask. "Vodka banishes the bad spirits." He offers the flask to Hedeon, who shakes his head. Bone-deep weariness washes over him.

"I assure you," Hedeon says, "it does not."

Orlov takes a swig and pockets the flask. "And in your *scientific opinion*," Orlov says, pointing at the ruined reactor, "how do we close that back up as soon as possible?"

Hedeon notices that the other men have joined them now, so Orlov must perform. Through his face shield, Orlov's assistant, Vasiliev, eyes him curiously. White light glitters across the surface of the pools.

"Containment must run simultaneously with evacuation," Hedeon says. He addresses the two new Party men. Perhaps higher-ups from Kiev will be more likely to listen to reason. Sofiya's face flashes in his mind.

He reminds himself that he is a dead man no matter what. His duty is to advocate for the truth.

"We need buses," he says. "Hundreds of them. Thousands. We need them yesterday. The priority must be to get our citizens out of Pripyat. Please." He glances from one man to the other, inscrutable behind their protective suits. "I'm begging you. Requisition all the vehicles you can in Kiev."

"Don't beg, Kozlov," Orlov says. His words are slurred. *He is more worried than he lets on,* Hedeon thinks. *The vodka is giving him liquid courage.* "It's unseemly of a man of your reputation. And you still haven't answered my question. How do we close it up?"

Hedeon glances at Vasiliev, then at the two Kiev apparatchiks.

"We'll handle the evacuation side of things," one of the men says. This does not inspire confidence in Hedeon.

"You tell us what to do about this." The second man points at the crumbled battlements of reactor number four, spewing icy light into the sky. Somewhere, a fireman shouts. Another replies. Something heavy crashes to the earth. Hedeon's head begins to ache, a pulsing tremor behind his eyes.

Hedeon turns to take in the full measure of ruin. He considers the early reports of his colleagues, and what he sees before him. His eyes travel across the expanse littered with graphite blocks spewed from the core, the firemen moving slowly among them like space explorers. Deep within the reactor, a red glow like the embers of coal behind a heating grate pulses with warmth and light.

"The core still burns," Hedeon says. "It must be close to one thousand degrees centigrade in there. And it will burn for months."

Orlov coughs into his hand. "So we'll put it out."

"Water or foam won't work," Hedeon continues. He pauses for a moment, thinking. "We could start with dolomite and lead. That might cool the fuel and quench the fire."

Orlov turns to the apparatchiks. "Can we requisition these things?"

"It will take some time," one of the men replies.

Orlov turns to Hedeon. "What can be done right now, at this moment, to get this under control?"

Hedeon shrugs. "I would need to speak with my colleagues."

"*Think*, Kozlov."

"Sand!" he blurts out. "We could drop sandbags on top of the reactor core. From helicopters. That should prevent a chain reaction, or at least slow it, for now, until we can determine more effective substances to drop on it."

"Good man!" Orlov claps him on the back. "Sand we can do."

"The Fifty-First Guards helicopter regiment is standing by," one of the apparatchiks says.

"Helicopters we can do, too!" Orlov nearly shouts with glee, as if he's the one coming up with the tactics to save the day.

"I still need to speak with my colleagues, urgently," Hedeon says. "I need to consult them on what, exactly, we should be dropping on the core. Besides sand."

"Fine!" Orlov says. Hedeon is grateful for the good mood that's suddenly taken hold of the man. Orlov turns to his assistant. "Get him to a phone, let him talk to the other eggheads, and *watch him*. Don't leave his side."

Vasiliev nods and beckons for Hedeon to follow him.

Hedeon hesitates. "Sir," he says to Orlov, "I urge you one more time to wear your mask."

Orlov lifts his flask. "Shut up, Kozlov."

CHAPTER
20

Vasiliev ushers Hedeon into a boxy little guardhouse jutting from a Chernobyl administration building. The room is empty except for a metal desk, upon which sits a telephone. He shuts the door behind them.

Alone in the small room, both men remove their masks and respirators.

"We cut the long-distance telephone lines for citizens of Pripyat," Vasiliev says.

"I know," Hedeon says wearily. "I just need to call around locally, to speak to a few of my—"

"*But*," Vasiliev interrupts, "we retained long-distance calling for official business."

He gazes pointedly at the phone on the desk.

"Oh," Hedeon says. He hesitates. "Um . . ."

Vasiliev rolls his eyes. "If one were to be left alone in here for a few minutes, one might be able to call whomever one chooses. And say anything he wishes."

Hedeon begins to understand.

"And the KGB?" His voice is hoarse.

Vasiliev shrugs. "There is nothing I can do about that. But if circumstances were desperate enough, and one thought the risk was warranted . . ."

"Yes," Hedeon says, heart quickening. "Yes, I understand."

Vasiliev puts on his mask. "I'll be right outside. Be quick about it."

After Orlov's assistant is gone, Hedeon takes a seat at the desk and lifts the phone to his ear. He thinks for a moment, then dials a Moscow number.

For a split second, a rush of anxiety nearly forces the phone back into its cradle.

It's a trick, he thinks. But he steels his resolve. So what if it is? There's nothing to lose at this point.

He wonders what a bullet to the back of the head feels like. If it's just abrupt darkness, a light blinking off and then a black void, or if there's a letting go, a gradual slipping away from everything he's ever loved . . .

"*Govorit Moskva.*" The greeting on the other end of the line is a cheeky one. *Moscow speaking* is the way the Party's radio broadcasts begin, every morning.

Hedeon can't help but smile, a little. "You haven't changed, old friend."

There's a pause. Then a shout. "Hedeon Kozlov! To what do I owe the honor of a phone call after—what's it been, an entire year since the conference in Minsk?"

"Two years, Vladimir. Twice the gray hairs."

"At least you still *have* hair, my friend. The ministry will make me lose what little I have left before long."

Vladimir Shasharin, deputy Soviet minister of energy, is an old university friend of Hedeon's.

"Listen to me, Vladimir—something's happened at Chernobyl."

"Yes, we've received reports of a small fire." He sounds surprised. "Is everything all right, Hedeon?"

"You know me. You know I don't play tricks. There is no political game here. I promise you, the situation is life or death."

There's a pause. "I understand, Hedeon. What is it that you need?"

"Buses—at least a thousand. Cars. Army trucks. Motorcycles. Anything that moves. We have to evacuate Pripyat as soon as possible, or everyone will die. And you're my only hope."

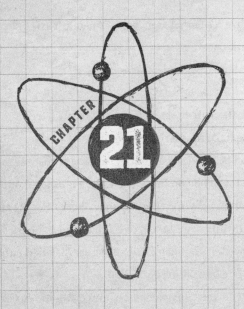

CHAPTER

21

Time is a funny thing, Yuri thinks.

"Funny, indeed," Sergei Federov, the trapped nuclear technician, says. "I remember when I was your age, and such things first
occurred to me. It's nice to feel like a philosopher, working out the universe's problems on your own. There's something pure about it. I miss those
days."

Yuri tries to think for a moment. Thinking has become hard to do, as if
his mind has been tossed a great distance away, and he must go on a quest
to find each new thought. "Did I say that out loud?"

There's a noise in the darkness like a wheezing cough. It takes Yuri a moment to realize it's Sergei's laughter. "You did, Yuri. Did you think I was reading your mind?"

Yuri thinks about this. Time passes.

And passes.

Here among the rubble, buried deep within the reactor, there is only darkness and heat. Darkness, heat, and time.

"What I mean is," Yuri says finally, "I'm always rushing to catch the bus to work, afraid I won't be on time. Then, time is *exact*—hours and minutes and seconds, bearing down on me. But now—here—time's smeared out into something totally different. Like how bubble gum is a hard stick, and then after being chewed, it's a mushy blob. But it's still called bubble gum. How can the same thing be so different?"

Another bout of wheezing laughter comes out of the darkness.

"You're going to make a wonderful atomschiki," Sergei says. "You've got a very rubbery mind."

Rubbery mind. Yuri thinks about this phrase for a long time. Or a short time—who can tell anymore?

Does radiation corrupt the passage of time like it corrupts the cells in the body?

He thinks about this.

Anyway, it's better than thinking about the wonderful atomschiki he's going to make, when he's no longer sure that this future self will ever come to be. In fact, this future self has become very dim and hard to make out. The future self that has been so clear, so vivid, ever since the day he watched the broadcast about the grand opening of Chernobyl.

There are other future selves, too, he realizes now. They've been there this whole time, looming in the background of his life. Even if he fails to become an atomschiki, there are other paths for Yuri Fomichev. A teacher, perhaps—an academician in one of the famed nuclear institutes. Or a schoolteacher in an atomgrad like Pripyat. His mind reels. There are other, stranger, far-flung selves, too—a fisherman on the Black Sea (because why not?), bringing the day's catch home to his wife . . .

Sofiya.

He closes his eyes. The darkness is the same.

Loneliness settles in his chest.

"Sergei!" he calls out as best he can.

Somewhere, rubble shifts with a groan. The vibrations send bright stabs of pain through his wrist and forearm.

He is connected to the heart of the Chernobyl-beast now, he thinks.

"Sergei!"

No answer.

Another future self takes shape in his mind—the one who didn't volunteer to squirm through narrow tunnels of wreckage to save a total stranger. The one who let the firemen escort him out of the plant. The one who is in the hospital right now, being treated. The one who is airlifted out of Pripyat, to rejoin the people he loves.

He opens his eyes.

The darkness is the same.

When Yuri first crawled into the tunnel, light came and went. It was bad light, to be sure—the sickly glow of graphite burning in the core, which would burn for months unless they figured out how to quell it.

If that light was reaching him, Yuri knew he was far too close to the core. But he had known that before he let Vasily lead him through the canyon of rubble.

Jagged edges of concrete and rebar scraped his skin.

The fact that it hurt less and less each time was the most troubling part.

He began to feel disconnected from himself.

Distant voices swirled around him like *rusalki* spirits and he swatted them away, convinced they weren't real.

Does radiation have a voice? A mind of its own? The brains of the Chernobyl-beast, spilled out over Pripyat?

"Sergei!" he managed to yell as he crawled.

"Over here!"

The trapped man's voice was louder now. Yuri nearly wept tears of joy. He was headed in the right direction! Perhaps this wouldn't be totally futile after all.

He drew hot air into his lungs. If not for this bodily disconnection, Yuri suspected the heat would be unbearable. This close to the burning core, even shielded by all this ruin, there was no hiding from it. The heat was a thick and stifling presence. If he were to crawl into the center of the core, he would be incinerated. The fact that Sergei was still responsive enough to call out meant that he was a safe enough distance away to avoid being burned to a crisp.

Although, after bathing in radiation, burning up might be a mercy.

"I'm coming to get you!" Yuri called out.

His voice was all odd angles and echoes.

Onward through the darkness.

He paused to vomit. Then he came to a dead end. The light was gone. He explored the space just ahead of him, running his hand along a dense wall of rubble. There were no gaps, not even a hole big enough for a mouse to squirm through. He considered turning around.

Then he realized there wasn't enough space for him to wriggle around and change direction.

He would have to crawl out backward.

Panic swelled and he began to cough. There wasn't enough air, it was all scorching and metallic, and he couldn't see a thing. He summoned saliva from his parched throat and spit to make sure he wasn't upside down.

He remembered reading about that trick in a book about surviving an avalanche.

It had been years ago, on an autumn Sunday, lying in his bed in the Moscow flat, the book open on his chest. Oh, to go back there now—to peace, normalcy, a mundane existence. He sent a message back to his younger self on that day, urging him to cherish the safety of his little bedroom, his covers, his pillow, his books . . .

Keep it together, Yuri.

Deep breaths. He waited until his heart stopped pounding. Then he called out.

"Sergei! I think I hit a dead end!"

"I'm over here!"

The voice was coming from off to the right, and several meters behind him. He had overshot. There was still hope.

"Keep talking!" he called out. Then he began to scuttle backward the way he came.

To Yuri's astonishment, Sergei begin to *sing*. It was weak and off-key—more a desperate chant—but Yuri recognized the words. It was the "Worker's Marseillaise," a revolutionary song every Soviet citizen knew by heart from childhood.

"Stand! Rise up, working people!"

Yuri stopped backtracking. Now Sergei was directly off to his right.

"Arise against the enemies, hungry brother!"

Yuri brought his knees to his chest and turned as best he could to face the direction of Sergei's raspy song.

"Let be heard the people's cry for vengeance!"

Yuri felt gently along the compressed rubble.

"Forward!"

He came to an opening. The air seemed cooler, fresher—he was facing away from the core! That was the first bit of good news he'd had since entering the tunnel. If Sergei was trapped closer to the core, they would be in danger of roasting alive.

"Forward!"

This part of the rubble maze was slightly more spacious. Instantly, Yuri felt more at ease. The claustrophobic, heart-pounding closeness of the last leg of his journey sloughed off him. He began to crawl faster. Here, he could almost walk in a low crouch. He felt as if he were going from the surface of the sun to a warm, relaxing bath. It was amazing how the body adapted, how what could be miserable at any other time became suddenly glorious in comparison.

"Forward!" Sergei was only a few meters away now. If it wasn't pitch-black, Yuri was sure he'd be able to see the man. Or, at least, whatever parts of him were visible through the collapsed concrete and steel.

"I'm almost there!" he called out.

Sergei began to laugh. Yuri joined in. They were going to get out of this. They were going to be Heroes of the Soviet Union. There would be triumph amid all this destruction. Perhaps he would begin to live up to his namesake, Yuri Gagarin. Perhaps—

The Chernobyl-beast shrieked.

All around him, rubble shifted. There was a terrible grinding. It was as if an earthquake was jostling the remains of the reactor.

"Yuri!" Sergei called above the din.

Instinctively, Yuri reached out a hand in the direction of Sergei's voice.

Then blinding pain shot up his arm. Hot compression gripped his hand, the sudden snapping-shut of a bear trap around his fingers. He screamed and the Chernobyl-beast screamed back.

The dark world settled with a groan. Something popped and flared in the distance.

Yuri's left arm was numb, yet on fire at the same time. But the heat wasn't pain, it was just an acknowledgment of the pain he would feel sometime later. Carefully, he tried to move his arm. Panic swelled. He tried to remain calm, to take stock of what had just happened. But panic had the upper hand. He wrenched his left shoulder back, trying to pull his arm free, and cried out at the jolt of pain that stabbed all the way down into his chest and stomach.

"Yuri!" Sergei cried out. "Are you all right?"

The man was so close, so maddeningly close!

Yuri tried to sound calm and in control, but his voice betrayed his distress. "I think—" He could barely get himself to say it. Speaking it aloud made it true. White cloudbursts exploded across his vision. "I think my hand is trapped."

As it turns out, it's only the index and middle fingers of his left hand that have been crushed between two chunks of concrete.

"Sergei!" he calls again.

"I'm here," the man says, and Yuri is flooded with relief. They have been speaking of time, and other things, trying to keep each other conscious.

Time is a piece of chewed gum that stretches away in every direction.

There is Yuri, face pressed to the TV screen.

For today, for today, current flows from the RBMK!

There is Yuri, on the railway bridge, handing a homemade dosimeter to Sofiya.

You made this yourself?

There is Yuri, watching his father stare out at the snowbanks, listening to his uncle speak treason at the dinner table, glowering at his cousins as they dance to American pop music.

The Talking Heads.

Chewing-gum time wraps around and around our lives, endlessly, binding our memories together.

Another one of his future selves blinks out of existence.

Pain is a dull ache. His left arm feels both too long and too short at the same time.

"Do you have a girlfriend?" Sergei's voice intrudes upon his scattered thoughts. An echo trails the words, as if the man has shouted into a canyon. Yuri is pretty sure his mind is playing a new trick.

"I don't know," Yuri says. "There's *someone*."

He wonders, for the first time, if Hedeon Kozlov would approve of him.

"Do you have a wife?" Yuri says.

"Yes," Sergei says. "Irina."

They are silent for a while.

"I need you to deliver a message to her," Sergei says.

Even in his haze, Yuri is startled. "Someone will come for us," he says. It doesn't sound convincing. "You can give her the message yourself."

Sergei wheezes. "Yuri. My friend. I won't make it."

Yuri tries to sing the Marseillaise to bolster the man's spirits, but the words turn to dust in his throat.

"You came to help me," Sergei says. "Now let me help you. You can move your right arm, yes?"

Yuri tests his right arm. It's sore, but it works. "Yes."

"Reach toward me. There's a small opening."

By now, his eyes have adjusted to the darkness, and he sees a black void the size of a workman's boot formed by the settling of the rubble. He extends his right arm and reaches through. His hand disappears. A moment later, he feels the heat of Sergei's hand.

He laughs out loud. "Sergei! It's you! We're this close!"

"Thick as thieves, as the Americans say."

Something metallic is pressed into Yuri's palm.

"Take it," Sergei says.

Yuri pulls his hand from the opening. He holds the object near his face. It's a folding pocketknife.

For a moment, he stares at it, dull and uncomprehending.

Then it dawns on him. What Sergei intends for him to do to free his fingers from the concrete.

His vision swims. His stomach flips. There is nothing left for him to vomit.

"I can't," he says weakly.

"Yes, you can," Sergei says. "Live to see your someone again."

CHAPTER 22

Night falls on eastern Ukraine.

The car—a mustard-colored Zhiguli pocked with rust and afflicted with an engine rattle—speeds west on the same road where, only this morning, the Kushnirs and the Fomichevs had sped east.

Reversing course. Heading for Pripyat.

"How much farther?" Alina raises her voice to be heard. The engine sounds like coins shaken in a tin can. She's buckled into the back seat alongside her brother, who's gazing quietly out the window. The sky is the deepest blue can get without fading entirely to black. Dark trees blur past. Pinprick lights in distant hills string lonely farmhouses together.

"About an hour," says the driver. His name is Nikolai. Alina guesses he's about thirty years old. Stylishly shaggy hair tufts from the sides of his peaked cap. He drives casually with one hand atop the wheel. A toothpick juts from his teeth. Every few miles, he tosses it out the window and replaces it with a fresh one. The toothpicks smell of mint.

For the hundredth time since they flagged down the passing car, Alina replays how they got here. She can scarcely believe it's because of actions *she* took, decisions *she* made.

Evading their parents had been easy enough in the dense woods behind the abandoned house.

What had been hard was hearing the desperation in her parents' voices as they scrambled through the trees, calling out *Alina!* and *Lev!* Even Fedir Kushnir had joined the search. But despite the urge to rush from her hiding place and jump into her father's arms, to ease his tension and fright, Alina's resolve to get back to Pripyat had only grown as she crouched in the underbrush.

If her parents got their way, Alina would never see Sofiya again. She and Lev would never know what happened to their cousin, Yuri.

She believes Yakiv Kushnir is telling the truth—that the accident at Chernobyl is very serious, and that Pripyat is dangerous. But Sofiya is the first friend she's ever had who's understood her, and helped her, and asked for nothing but friendship in return. Living elsewhere—even if it's much safer than Pripyat—without knowing what happened to Sofiya is no life at all.

She is certain it was Sofiya she saw out the window of the van, melting into the darkness of Lenina Prospekt.

Back there in the woods, Alina didn't know if what she was doing was *right*, exactly—in fact, it troubled her greatly that it might be very wrong—but the nagging, clawing sensation gripping her mind began to fall away and dissolve as she focused on the path back to Pripyat.

At dusk, it had been a simple matter to pop out of the forest a kilometer or so down the road from the farmhouse and hail passing cars. Eventually, one of them stopped for the two kids with overstuffed backpacks on the side of an empty road.

A mustard-colored Zhiguli, driven by a young man named Nikolai, heading west toward Pripyat.

"Tell me again what it looked like," Nikolai says. He has the curiosity of an eager student. He might be an atomschiki himself, Alina thinks—he hasn't said much about what he does for a living.

"Like an alien death ray," Lev says. "A giant laser beam shooting up into the sky."

Nikolai whistles. It makes Alina think of a cowboy in an American western movie.

"And you're heading *back* to all this."

"We're not going to stay for long," Alina says. "We just have to find my friend. And our cousin."

"Well, you two are just about the bravest kids I ever met."

Alina glances at her brother. Lev meets her eyes. She tries to read his mood. Everything happened so fast—their narrow escape from Fedir in the backyard, fleeing madly through the woods, hiding from their parents, flagging down a car—that Alina didn't have a chance to ask Lev if he was all right. He had simply followed her lead. She tries to squash rising guilt. What has she led her little brother into? Would he be better off back at the farmhouse?

What if they'd both be better off?

Suddenly, Alina feels very alone. The Ukrainian countryside is impossibly vast. She wishes Sofiya were here.

"Do you have any snacks?" Lev says abruptly.

Nikolai laughs. "I didn't pack any food. Didn't plan on heading all the way to Pripyat this evening." Alina watches his eyes in the rearview mirror. They flick to the back seat. "Can I interest you in a toothpick?"

"No, thanks," Lev says, and turns back to the world outside as the final traces of dusk are swallowed up by the night.

"What do you do, Nikolai?" Alina says. With an hour to go, she might as well make polite conversation. Besides, sitting in silence gives her thoughts the space to run free, making it easy for the nagging feeling to overwhelm her. She wonders what Nikolai would think if she put on her headphones and listened to music.

"Oh, a little of this and a little of that," he says.

Alina doesn't know how to respond to that. It's a strange answer: Everyone in the Soviet Union has a job. She has always been taught that unemployment is an American problem. If you refuse to work in the Soviet Union, you are labeled a "parasite," and shipped off to the kinds of places parents warn their lazy children about.

She doubts that Nikolai is a parasite. How could he afford this car, and the petrol to fuel it?

Could Nikolai be a KGB agent? That might explain his evasiveness.

"What does your father do?" he asks in return.

"He's the voice of Radio Pripyat," Lev says. "Everybody in the whole city knows him."

"Do they now?" Nikolai's gaze flits once again to the rearview. At the same time, he tosses his toothpick out the window. "Alina, is your brother exaggerating? Or am I really playing chauffeur to the children of a celebrity?"

"He's not exaggerating," Alina says. "Our father's on the radio."

"Hmm," Nikolai says. "The voice of Radio Pripyat. You know, I might have heard him myself, once or twice."

He turns around to look at Alina and Lev over the top of the headrest. His hand remains on the wheel. The car barrels down the highway.

Nikolai grins. "I bet you've got some really nice things tucked away in that empty apartment. I wouldn't mind a little tour."

"Can you please watch the road?" Alina says.

Headlights appear in the opposite lane, growing larger. Big and bright—*a truck.* The Zhiguli drifts over the center line.

Nikolai doesn't budge. "What do you say? You want to show me around? Let me see all those leather-bound books?"

"Watch out!" Lev yells.

The truck blares its horn. Nikolai's grin broadens, his snaggle-toothed smile seeming to fill up his face. "What do you say?!" he yells in return. "What do you say?!"

"Yes!" Alina says. "Please just—"

Nikolai whips his head around to face the road and jerks the wheel. The Zhiguli slides back into its proper lane. The truck speeds past.

"Thank you," Nikolai says. "I'm really looking forward to it. It won't be long now . . ."

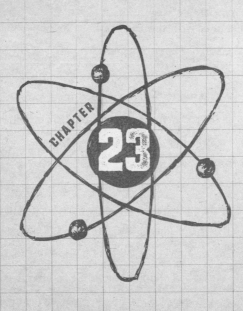

CHAPTER 23

*P*onderous. *The chimes of a clock.*

Lines from Mayakovsky zip through her mind. Sofiya, clad in a wrinkly, mothball-scented protective suit she found in her father's closet, wishes she still had her dosimeter. The numbers would be glowing red in the darkness of the forest. What would the reading be? She is still a full kilometer from the shrub. Avoiding the militsiya checkpoint had forced her to stay off the road and bushwhack straight through the woods south of the city.

Everything is a clock, she thinks. The dosimeter counts up. Life counts down.

After her encounter with the Forgettable Man, she tried to follow her own advice and stay in her home. She really did. But the KGB agent's words followed her—*Yuri Fomichev is still inside the plant, people do get lost, it happens all the time*—and resounded in the silence of her empty apartment. She thought of Alina as she paced from room to room. She wondered if this anxious, distracted state was how her friend felt all the time.

This nearly brought her to tears.

Sofiya doesn't know what she'll do when she gets to the shrub. It's dangerous, foolhardy, and quite possibly deadly to be headed in this direction, toward that icy pillar that's once again spearing the night. Patches of glowing sky come and go through the trees.

Sofiya feels as if she has slipped her skin and wriggled into someone else's body. How easy it is for everything to change, and change again! It's not merely that life is fragile—her mother could be *here* one minute and *gone* the next—but the plans we make, the paths we plot, all of it so easily thrown off course.

A hat, blown off her father's head and carried by the wind to the Fomichevs at the riverside.

A boy from Moscow, suddenly appearing in her life.

Some combination of human error and bad luck at Chernobyl, and the city of Pripyat is poisoned forever.

All this has convinced Sofiya that there's no point in sitting and waiting for things to get worse.

She will go to the shrub, and if there's something to be done to help, she will do it.

For Yuri.

For her father.

Branches whip and slide against the thin plastic of her protective suit.

She doesn't dare use a flashlight for fear of attracting militsiya—or the Forgettable Man, that soft-spoken KGB agent who seems to be everywhere and nowhere. Pripyat is a haunted place, she realizes now—but instead of being haunted by ghosts, it's haunted by men. All of them creeping through shadows of their own making.

Ponderous. The ticks of a clock.

Ticktock.

Ticktock.

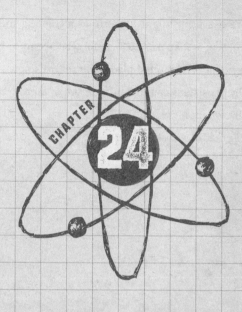

CHAPTER

24

26 APRIL 1986
8:49 P.M.

The Zhiguli bounces along the empty back roads. Nikolai skirts the northern edge of the Kiev Reservoir—an even blacker void in the darkness. In the back seat, Alina holds her brother's hand. She doesn't dare lean over to whisper to him.

The thought of this man with his nightmare grin running roughshod through their neat and lovely apartment, tearing books from the shelves and smashing lamps, has filled her with despair.

This is all her fault.

Part of her wishes she had left her brother behind, so he'd be safe at the farmhouse with their parents.

Another part of her is glad he's here with her, so she isn't alone with Nikolai.

"I'm just a normal person," he says cheerfully. "You don't have to be afraid of me."

Alina and Lev remain silent.

"I have a mother, a father, and two older sisters," he says. The car skips across a pothole. The engine protests with a series of alarming clanks. "I've never hurt anyone before. I don't even kill spiders, or swat flies, or slap mosquitos. Do you believe me?"

Nikolai curses under his breath as the car squeals around a sharp bend in the road.

"Do you?" he asks again.

"Yes," Alina says quietly.

"Good," he says. "I don't want you to be scared. Besides, just think—you could have been picked up by anyone, but fate threw us together. Maybe it happened for a reason, you know? I'd like to have children of my own some-day. A boy and a girl. That's perfect. Tell me, do you live in one of those massive apartment blocks?"

Silence from the back seat.

"Ah, well," Nikolai continues as if this is a pleasant conversation, "I guess I'll find out soon enough. I bet *the voice of Radio Pripyat* keeps some vodka on hand. I bet it's the good stuff, too."

As the car emerges from the cover of thick foliage that forms a leafy tunnel, the sky turns from starless black to an icy blush.

Alina's first thought is *They still haven't fixed it*.

She squeezes her brother's hand.

Nikolai whistles. He cranes his neck as he drives, to stare up at the painted sky.

"Unbelievable," he says. "Alien death ray! I can really see that. Good description, kid. You think it's—"

There's a tremendous *bang* as the car jolts to a sudden halt. Alina's teeth clamp down on the tip of her tongue. Her eyes water and she tastes blood. Nikolai's head whips forward and back. His forehead smacks the top of the steering wheel.

He cries out, cursing. He stomps on the gas pedal. The tires spit dirt. The engine rattles. The car doesn't move.

Alina squeezes her brother's hand, hard. She meets his eyes in the darkness. Wordlessly, they agree.

Leaving their heavy backpacks behind, they unbuckle their seat belts, unlock the doors, and hit the ground running. Out the corner of her eye, Alina sees a fallen tree blocking the road. The front of the Zhiguli is crumpled up against it.

"Head for the light," Alina says. Lev falls in beside her. "Maybe he won't follow us there."

But a moment later, Nikolai is screaming for them to stop, running after them. Alina risks a glance over her shoulder. He's just barely visible, touched ever so slightly by the light in the sky. And he's gaining on them.

"This way," she tells her brother. Together they leave the road and go crashing through the underbrush. Everything falls away—her parents, Fedir Kushnir, the farmhouse, hiding in the woods, flagging down a mustard-colored Zhiguli. There's only the blood-rush in her ears, the sound of her brother breathing hard at her heels—and right behind them both, gaining fast—

Nikolai.

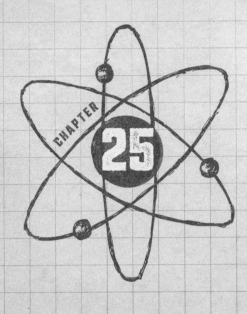

CHAPTER

25

Hedeon has rejoined Leonid Orlov and the Party bosses from Kiev. They are all of them—even Orlov and Vasiliev—scooping up sand from the banks at the northern edge of the coolant reservoir, filling sandbag after sandbag. The fire brigades pitch in. Even with a dozen men working together, Hedeon thinks, the number of filled sandbags is pathetically small.

As he works, he tries not to look at the smoking ruin of the reactor. But he can't help it.

They will need thousands of sandbags. Maybe even millions.

He takes comfort in knowing that Vladimir Shasharin, his contact in

Moscow, is pulling the proper strings to get the evacuation underway.

He has done what he could for the city.

Now he must fill sandbags for the reactor.

The work is methodical. Despite his aching limbs, Hedeon feels a small measure of peace. Sofiya is tugging at his thoughts, but at least now he knows that she will be evacuated from the poisoned city.

Suddenly, he is aware of a furtive presence. A man slinks out of the darkness and goes to Orlov's side. The man is not wearing any protective gear—not even a mask. Hedeon takes his hands out of the dirt.

The man is Ivanov, the KGB agent who hovered over the proceedings in the conference room at the White House. He speaks to Orlov quietly.

Both men glance in his direction.

Hedeon stands up straight. *It's time,* he thinks wearily. *I'm finished.*

Orlov and the KGB agent stride down the row of firemen and Party bosses filling sandbags. Hedeon awaits them quietly. A peculiar stillness takes over. He gazes up at the pillar of light and doesn't lower his eyes until the two men are standing right in front of him.

"Kozlov," Orlov says, "what have you done?"

Hedeon blinks. Orlov sounds genuinely sad.

The KGB agent regards him implacably. Then he takes a small tape recorder from the inside pocket of his suit jacket. He presses a button. Hedeon's own voice fills the air. The clarity of the recording is remarkable. He hears himself speak to Vladimir Shasharin.

"Buses—at least a thousand. Cars. Army trucks. Motorcycles. Anything that moves. We have to evacuate Pripyat as soon as possible, or everyone will die. And you're my only—"

Ivanov clicks a button. Hedeon's voice ceases.

Hope, Hedeon thinks, finishing the thought.

"You fool," Orlov says. He shakes his head and mutters something under his breath.

Hedeon stays quiet. What is there to say? What's done is done.

Ivanov pockets the tape recorder. His hand stays hidden inside his jacket.

Orlov puts a fatherly hand on Hedeon's shoulder and looks him in the eyes. "I can't stop what's going to happen now, Kozlov," he says.

Hedeon swallows the lump in his throat. "Sofiya."

Orlov nods. "I'll do what I can." He squeezes Kozlov's shoulder. *"You damned fool."*

Orlov holds his gaze for a second longer, then lowers his arm and turns away.

Ivanov pulls his hand from his jacket. The hand holds a pistol.

"Hedeon Kozlov," he says softly. "Please turn around and get down on your knees."

Hedeon turns to face away from the KGB agent. The command is fine with him—to have this man, and the barrel of his PSM pistol, be the last thing Hedeon ever sees is an ending he would rather avoid.

Yet he does not kneel. He stands and takes in the world, such as it is. Off to his right, the ruined reactor expels its glittering poison. Firemen and militsiya in gauze surgical masks handle great chunks of irradiated graphite. Even through his suit, Hedeon can taste the metal in the air. The deadly particles.

Straight ahead is a view into the darkened forest that surrounds the plant. This, he decides, will be the last thing he sees. A strange calm settles over him. He has done what he could. What is one man against the slippery whims, backroom deals, and brutal disregard of State and Party? There are so many like him, crushed to dust and blown away. Scattered to the Soviet winds. And there will be many more to come.

He raises his face shield and removes his respirator. It no longer matters. He just wants to see.

"Get down on your knees." Ivanov repeats the order.

Here come my last words, Hedeon thinks. He wonders if anyone will hear them and remember, or if they will be lost to time. "I prefer to stand."

There is a long pause. Then he feels the barrel of the gun against the back of his head. "That is acceptable," Ivanov says.

Hedeon Kozlov opens his heart to whatever comes next. Whatever comes afterward.

Several things happen at once.

Figures emerge from the forest. Two—no, three—coming straight at him. A fourth, too, off to his left. And to the right, out of the corner of his eye, a *fifth* figure emerges from the ruins of the plant.

Hedeon decides he's already been shot, rocketed across the bridge to an afterlife that looks remarkably similar to the world he just left. He didn't feel a thing, but he supposes a bullet to the brain would be relatively painless.

You're here one second, and gone the next. Just like that.

And the figures? Relatives. Ancestors. Long-lost loved ones, he guesses. Which means, perhaps, that one of them is his wife.

He bears himself up straight to meet her.

That's when he hears the screaming that seems to come from every direction at once.

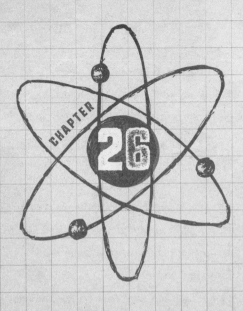

CHAPTER

26

Alina bursts from the trees, Lev at her side, and the hulking ruin of the power plant nearly stops her in her tracks. The icy glow sends rippling patterns across the coolant reservoir, unfurling darkly just ahead.

"Look!" shouts Lev.

A man in protective gear (though without a helmet or face shield) stands very still, facing them, and Alina is hit by the sensation that she knows him—and that he's staring right at her.

A man wearing a suit is standing just behind him, raising a pistol to the back of his head.

An execution?

She doesn't know which way to turn, or where to run. There are so many people, so much activity—militsiya, firemen, apparatchiks, men filling sandbags on the banks of the reservoir.

And she is not the only one running. A figure has emerged from the wreckage of the plant, sprinting toward the reservoir. He is shredding his throat, screaming nonsense.

At the same time, Alina is conscious of the pounding footsteps behind her. Nikolai's pursuit has not wavered.

As light bathes the sprinting, screaming figure coming from the ruins, Alina sees the tattered white uniform, the blistered and bloody face, the wild eyes—and the sight spurs her on, even faster.

"Yuri!" she calls out in disbelief.

Her cousin does not look her way. Instead, he launches himself at the man with the gun.

Time slows. Yuri seems to hang in the air, arms outstretched.

At the moment Yuri collides with the gunman, a pistol shot rings out. The man in the protective gear flinches as if he's been shot. Now Alina is close enough to recognize him. Her mind, struck by so many new things at once, flashes his name at her: Hedeon Kozlov!

Alina hears—and *feels*—the gunman's shot go wide, missing his target entirely. The bullet zips past her ear. Her head swivels around, spun as if attached to the bullet's wake.

Behind her, Nikolai cries out. The stray shot cuts his legs out from under him and he flips into the air and hits the ground hard.

Alina and Lev race toward their cousin, who is pummeling the man in the suit, fists hammering the man's face. One of his hands is slick with blood—it's as if he's dipped it in dark red paint. That bloody fist looks awkward and wrong, strangely incomplete.

As Alina arrives at the edge of the reservoir, it's her brother who first realizes that someone else—a girl she hasn't yet seen—has joined them. Lev tugs at his sister's sleeve and points.

Alina can scarcely believe it. She feels like she's going to pass out. The world seems to expand and contract around her, and she has the impression of being inside a snow globe beneath a glowing, starless sky.

Even behind the surgical mask hastily fastened to her face with cellophane, the girl is easy to recognize.

"Sofiya!" Alina says.

But Sofiya scarcely seems to see her friend. Alina follows her gaze. Like a clock in desperate need of winding, the mechanics driving Yuri grind to a halt. He flails one last fist into the gunman's battered face, then collapses in a heap at his side.

Only then does Alina see her cousin fully for the first time.

She is aware that she is crying out at the sight of his raw, blistered flesh. And Yuri's hand, the hand that used to sketch precise geometric patterns in his little notebook, is missing two of its fingers.

Yuri's eyes stare sightlessly up into the night sky.

People begin to gather. Men in dark suits. An air of authority surrounds them. *Party bosses,* Alina thinks.

Sofiya rushes to Yuri's side.

"Stay back!" her father, Hedeon, warns. But she ignores him and kneels down to press a hand against the side of his face.

"Kozlov," one of the Party bosses says. But Hedeon ignores him, and the man seems unsure of what to say next.

Hedeon kneels down, lifts Yuri's limp body in his arms, and stands up straight.

"I am taking this boy to the hospital," he announces. The Party bosses stare at him. No one makes a move to stop him.

"I know where there's a car," Alina says, glancing back at Nikolai's prone body. "It hit a tree, but it might still work."

Hedeon regards her. He doesn't seem surprised to see her. He seems like he's been expecting her. "All right," he says.

Alina is about to turn and lead them all toward the Zhiguli's resting place in the woods, when Sofiya rushes toward her. The next thing she knows, Alina is being wrapped in the tightest hug she's ever received. The constant nagging in her mind, the madness of the past twenty-four hours, all melts away. She hugs her friend back as fiercely as she can. Sofiya's body trembles. She is weeping.

Put the hurt on me, Alina thinks. *I can help you bear it.*

She says this out loud and adds, "I always will."

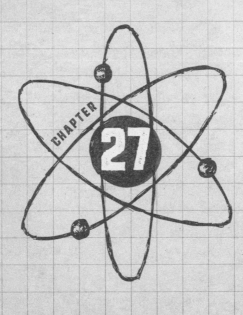

CHAPTER

27

H a!" Hedeon Kozlov shouts. The Zhiguli's engine sputters and catches with a growl. The crumpled hood sheds bits of rust as the car shudders to life and backs away from its resting place against the fallen tree. Only one headlight comes on, a single beam to sweep the dark woods. Hedeon cranks the wheel to turn around.

Cyclops, Alina thinks, her wired mind catching the stray thought.

She's stuffed into the back seat between Sofiya and Lev. Sofiya's hug hasn't yet ended: She and Alina cling to each other, making up for time apart.

The Zhiguli bounces along the dirt road.

"Built like a tank!" Hedeon exclaims, gripping the wheel with both hands, leaning forward in his seat to peer through the windshield. It's as if some alien energy has invaded the body of Sofiya's father, a man Alina has always known as taciturn and measured. Even in the aftermath of his would-be execution, he'd been matter-of-fact, proceeding calmly. Now he slaps the steering wheel. "Ha!" he shouts again. The car skids through a sharp turn.

"That's Soviet industry for you." It takes Alina a moment to register that the hushed voice belongs to Yuri.

Sofiya darts forward to reach for the boy in the front seat.

"You shouldn't touch me," Yuri says. Sofiya brushes her fingertips against his shoulder, a split second of contact, then lowers her hand. "My father drives a Zhiguli," Yuri continues. "It's the color of a . . . pomegranate." His voice is a whisper, dry as dust. Alina can hear the fire in his throat, the struggle to get each word out. "It's so ugly." He begins to laugh. The hoarse, choking sound brings tears to her eyes.

The car's single headlight slides across dense woods, winding path, then woods again. The road, such as it is, is longer and more twisty than Alina recalls from their mad journey with Nikolai.

Yuri stops laughing. His body goes limp in the front seat. The car hits a bump and he bounces like a rag doll.

"Keep him talking!" Hedeon says.

"I stole half your Vzletnaya lemon candies!" Lev blurts out. "I'm really sorry, but they were just sitting there in the bag on your dresser, and it didn't seem like you ever ate them, so I figured you wouldn't miss one or two. Per day. I'm sorry, Yuri. I'll buy you more. And if you don't like candy, I'll buy you something else. A book! Something you'd like, a super-boring one!"

Yuri's body jolts. He doubles over in his seat, racked with a coughing fit. He brings a hand to his mouth and Alina catches a glimpse of the stumps where two of his fingers used to be. She looks away.

Hedeon curses and jams his foot down on the gas pedal. The engine protests, and the car rockets from the dirt path. They careen out of the woods onto a real road. The tires grip smooth pavement. Pripyat's southern sprawl comes up fast, apartment blocks rising in the night. They're less than a kilometer away.

"I know you don't like American music," Alina says, "but maybe you could take me to a concert in Moscow someday? My parents would let me go if I went with you. They love you."

Yuri unfolds himself and sits up straight in his seat. "Moscow," he says dreamily. He closes his eyes. "My father stares at the snowbanks. You're lucky. You and Lev."

"I wish you could have met my mother," Sofiya says. "She would have loved you, too."

"Yes," Hedeon says. "She would have."

"She played guitar," Sofiya says. "Classical. Segovia was her favorite."

Yuri mutters something. Sofiya and Alina lean forward.

"Sergei's wife . . ." Now Yuri's voice is thin and wispy. "Irina. I have to tell her . . ." He trails off.

"It's okay," Sofiya says. "We're almost there. Hang on, Yuri."

Up ahead, a militsiya truck is parked across both lanes, blocking the road.

Hedeon slows. He slams his palm against the Zhiguli's feeble horn. The truck doesn't move.

Alina gives Lev a nudge. He rolls down his window and leans out. "Help!" he shouts. "We need help over here!"

A young soldier steps into view, startled, shielding his eyes with a hand.

Not much older than Yuri, Alina thinks.

"Hang on," Sofiya says. "You have to hang on."

The soldier begins to jog toward the car.

"You want to know a secret?" Yuri whispers. Alina finds Sofiya's hand and squeezes it.

"Yes," Sofiya says, "then I'll tell you one of mine."

The soldier stops at Hedeon's window and shines his flashlight inside the car.

The beam catches Yuri slumped in the front seat, laughing softly to himself. "I think I do like the Talking Heads."

EPILOGUE

AN EXCERPT FROM THE MEMOIRS OF SOFIYA KOZLOV APRIL 2021

That night, I turned my back on the Chernobyl nuclear power plant and its devastated reactor number four, and I never saw it again.

Now it's a destination for adventurous tourists. Americans and Europeans pay guides ($100 US if they book in advance, last I checked) to escort them through a power plant, and a city, frozen in time—decayed, yes, but also startlingly intact. Classroom desks, abandoned toys, faded murals. The amusement park's bumper cars, haphazardly parked as if they had just stalled out between rides a moment ago. Empty pools, discarded strollers, swing sets. The six-foot statue of Prometheus, who gave fire to mankind, still standing triumphantly in front of the cinema, holding his flames aloft.

The stuff of our lives, things we once loved, now used as bait for likes and comments in people's Instagram feeds. Everything we left behind forever, artfully composed into neat little squares.

Hollywood made a horror movie there, too.

Anyway.

There are things I've always wondered. Things I'll never know.

Is the tree that fell across the road through the woods and saved Alina and Lev still there? Does some of the glass from the Zhiguli's smashed headlights still glitter in the dirt?

Is there some remnant of that militsiya blockade at the edge of Pripyat, an oil smudge from the truck, a print from the sole of that young soldier's boot?

I remember my father's insistence, as the soldier leaned down and shone his flashlight into our faces: "This boy is going to die unless you let us through."

Hospital 126, where they were taking all the Chernobyl victims, was well inside the city limits.

But the soldier had his orders: no one in, no one out. Pripyat was sealed up tight. And a member of the militsiya wasn't going to think for himself. He was going to call a superior, who was going to call someone in Kiev, and on, and on.

So that's what happened. Time passed. The night wore on. We sat in the car.

Eventually, Yuri died. Maybe it would have been too late for him, either way. I'll never know.

In the years that followed, whenever I was feeling bad, a thought would get stuck in my head, and I would feel even sorrier for myself:

I never got a chance to really know him.

Yuri and I had the beginning of something, and it is still precious to me. Even through the hazy lens of the three decades that have passed, I maintained that our fleeting courtship, in the brief time we were given, was indeed very beautiful, and pure. It was taken away far too soon.

Later, I began to realize that this was selfish—rooted more in self-pity than anything else. Because the real tragedy wasn't the snuffing-out of a little fling that may or may not have lasted beyond Yuri's internship at the plant. The real tragedy was the absence of the person he could have been—a boy already capable of making a working dosimeter. A boy with vision, drive, and intelligence. A boy who was kind, in his own strange way. What would he have done with those gifts?

It's something else I often wonder.

Now I will write no more of Yuri Fomichev. Not because I have forgotten him—that will never happen—but because I have chosen to write no more of death.

Mayakovsky wrote, *I myself feel like a Soviet factory, manufacturing happiness.*

I don't believe my words can truly manufacture happiness from the raw material of such a catastrophe. But so much has already been written of Chernobyl, and its deadly aftermath, that I wish now to write only of life and its continuation rather than its abrupt and terrible conclusion.

On Sunday, April 27, 1986, the order finally came for Pripyat to be evacuated—a full day and a half after the explosions that rocked the power plant made the city forever uninhabitable. Moscow TV at last acknowledged the accident; State-run radio played only classical music. Meanwhile, 1,225 buses and 250 trucks and other vehicles collected the citizens of Pripyat from 160 apartment buildings.

I was among them, along with Alina and Lev.

My father was not. He was detained at the militsiya checkpoint—and then transferred to police custody, though I would not know that until much later—while Alina, Lev, and I were ushered into the city and allowed to return to the Fomichevs' apartment. There, exhausted, we sprawled about the living room and caught a few hours' sleep.

Around lunchtime the next day, we were urged to pack some food and a few personal belongings, and join the crowds waiting to board the buses. (Lev, I will always remember, stuffed an entire knapsack with chocolates, so he had no room for a change of clothes.) Nobody seemed to care, or even notice, that we were unattended by our parents. We were simply three more little bodies among the hundred thousand evacuees.

An entirely different book could be written about our arrival in one of the villages near Kiev, about the family that took the three of us in, and about how Pavlo and Mayya Fomichev eventually tracked us down. It would have many chapters about the unfair scapegoating of my father, and the eventual begrudging admission, by the Party, that he had acted heroically. (This came too late to save his career, of course.) The Fomichevs would get their own section, too: about how Pavlo was stripped of his Party membership and never allowed behind another radio microphone again; about how Mayya kept the family together through the hard times that followed her husband's fall from grace.

I know I vowed to write no more of death, but I should mention that Yakiv Kushnir was tried and executed for fleeing his post. I never learned what happened to Fedir.

Alina and I remain the best of friends. She lives down the street from me still, in Moscow, and our families (we each have a boy and a girl) vacation together every year at a dacha by the Black Sea.

Now, I know what you're thinking: What about radiation sickness, cancer, birth defects? The lingering aftereffects of exposure to that open reactor core that afflicted so many?

Well, you can read about all that online. I won't speak of it here, except to tell you that Alina and I both fared better than some, and worse than others, in that regard.

But we're both still alive. And our children are healthy.

In fact, I'm looking over the top of my laptop at Alina at this very moment, as I write these words from the porch of the dacha. She doesn't know I'm watching her as she walks slowly back to the house from the beach, where she has been collecting seashells. It's one of the many activities we have discovered over the years to help calm her mind. Now, after so much time, it's as if we've switched roles.

She, the renowned psychiatrist, an example of stillness, contentment, and calm for her patients.

I, the less-renowned writer, jittery with nerves and coffee.

As she climbs the steps to the porch, she places her hand on my shoulder and pretends to read what I'm writing. I have to snap the laptop closed.

I know better than to try to speak to her. She'll have to take off her headphones first, pause the song, and pretend to be annoyed at the interruption.

She lingers for a moment, looking out at the sea, and I can hear the muffled sounds of the Talking Heads. Alina Fomichev loves her American music.

We glance at each other and trade smiles. Then I decide to interrupt her anyway. I point at my ears. She rolls her eyes—exaggeratedly—and takes off her headphones.

"I'm writing about that night," I tell her. There's no need to specify which one. She'll know exactly what I'm talking about. "And it turns out you were right."

"Oh," she says. "Well, that's good. I enjoy being right."

"I mean when you said 'I always will.' Do you remember?"

She gives my shoulder a squeeze. *"Put the hurt on me,"* she quotes herself from memory. *"I can help you bear it."*

"And you always did."

THE END

AUTHOR'S NOTE

The main characters in this book never really existed. However, it's my hope that their fictional exploits do some justice to the very real lives lived by the citizens of Pripyat—both the remarkable and the ordinary men, women, and children who inspired the Fomichevs, the Kozlovs, and their little universe of friends and enemies.

The exceptions are Toptunov and Akimov, the power plant operators who team up with Yuri for their doomed quest to open the valves. Obviously, their dialogue and actions have been invented to serve the scenes with Yuri, but I included them to pay tribute to everyone who exhibited great bravery or simply did the best they could under impossible circumstances. In real life, Toptunov and Akimov both died of radiation poisoning in the weeks following the disaster. They weren't recognized for their heroism until 2008, when they were awarded (posthumously) the Ukrainian Order for Courage, Third Class.

I'd never know about the avoska—the "what-if" bag for grocery shopping—or a thousand other elements of Soviet life without the detailed reporting and storytelling of several great authors. I relied on their scrupulous research to breathe as much life as I could into this book, and I'd like to give them the credit they deserve. I recommend the following books to anyone interested in reading more about the real story of Chernobyl and the people who lived and died in its shadow.

I'm fortunate that *Midnight in Chernobyl* by Adam Higginbotham came out in the months before I started researching this book. It's perfect for anyone looking for a tense, minute-by-minute account of the disaster, along with a brilliant examination of the operation of the plant (from its construction onward), the science behind those massive Soviet reactors, and the behavior of everyone involved. Similarly, *Chernobyl: History of a Tragedy* by Serhii Plokhy is filled with a wealth of incredible detail. Together, the two books provide a wonderfully comprehensive view of the event and its aftermath from every angle, from the human to the scientific.

I relied heavily on *Soviet Society Today* ("today" as in 1989, when the book was published) by Michael Rywkin for information about everything from Soviet ideology and culture to the habits of Soviet kids. This book also provided a valuable tour through the systems that made up Soviet society— wages, jobs, housing, education, the Party. Not to mention dissent.

Finally, I have to cite *Voices from Chernobyl* by Svetlana Alexievich. This oral history examines the impact of Chernobyl on people's lives in the form of haunting monologues and is essential reading for anyone interested in real human stories from that time and place.

While I drew on these books to ground this story in a realistic setting, I took liberties with both the timeline of events and the layout of the city of Pripyat to better suit these characters' specific adventures. Beyond that, any glaring historical errors should be blamed on me and not the authors mentioned here.

Oh, and *"For today, for today, current flows from the RBMK!"* is apparently a real song. If anybody has a copy of that one, I'd love to hear it.

ABOUT THE AUTHOR

Andy Marino is the author of the Plot to Kill Hitler trilogy and several other novels for young readers. He currently lives in upstate New York. You can visit him at andy-marino.com.